CALIFORNIA
MAN

Carole Dean

A KISMET™ Romance

METEOR PUBLISHING CORPORATION
Bensalem, Pennsylvania

Always Tim.
And Pat, my sister and best friend.

CAROLE DEAN

Carole lives in British Columbia. Recently she became an island dweller—and loves it. Every morning she wakes to the ever-changing sound and colors of the ocean outside her window. Whatever its mood, summer calm or winter storm, she finds it the perfect background for writing romance. She lives with her husband of many years and a Rhodesian Ridgeback who has convinced them both he is a person in dog's clothing.

Other books by Carole Dean:

No. 89   *JUST ONE KISS*

ONE

Quinn Ramsay stood on the foredeck of the ferry staring at the island of his retreat. It was small, green, and tranquil—and it was a long way from L.A.

Six weeks. What the hell was he going to do here for six long weeks?

He zipped up his jacket, stuffed his hands into the pocket of his slacks, and shrugged his broad shoulders, the act half in resignation to his immediate future and half in defense against the cool wind blowing through the narrow channel.

What was it Paul called this place? . . .

Paul was enthusiastic. "Salt Spring Island is a jewel, Quinn, a real jewel. You'll love it. There's cycling, hiking, scuba diving, and some damn fine fishing. I'm sure you can find something to occupy yourself."

"I'll pass on the fishing, thanks, but the cycling sounds like a good idea—and maybe the hiking. I could use the time to get in shape." He made a mental note to pick up a couple of mountain bikes from his local Action Sports Store.

Paul Severns looked across the lunch table at his friend and chuckled. "Yeah, you're falling to pieces, big guy. Anyone can see that." At six feet two inches and just under two hundred pounds, Quinn Ramsay was in perfect physical condition. "The star of my latest picture should look so good," Paul finished.

"Maybe so, but the last six months have been nothing but one damned meeting and one jet after another. I've spent so much time in elevators, offices, and underground parking lots, I'm beginning to feel like a caged chicken."

Quinn looked out at the beach in front of his Malibu home. His gaze slid disinterestedly over a perfectly sculptured California body, then down to his watch. *Relax*, he told himself. *It's Sunday afternoon. Your schedule is clear until tonight.* Then? Another plane to catch. He was sick to death of his schedule. He returned his level blue gaze to Paul. "So tell me more about this island jewel."

"It's off the coast of Vancouver Island in British Columbia. I found out about it from a guy on the lighting crew when we were shooting in Vancouver a couple of years ago. He grew up there. He took a bunch of us fishing and it was fantastic! I caught a fifteen-pound sockeye that—"

Quinn stared down his friend, daring him to continue with his fish story.

"Okay, okay, so fishing's not on your A list. Anyway, as a place to mull things over, it'll be perfect. I think the population is seven, maybe eight thousand. There's no night life to speak of." Paul spotted the bikini and paused to take a drink and a look. Quinn's deck made for some blue-ribbon beach watching. He continued, "I guess the best word to describe it is peaceful."

Quinn grimaced. He wasn't big on peaceful.

"My place is on the waterfront at the north end. The whole island can't be more than twenty miles in length, so it doesn't take long to get anywhere. There's a caretaker and his wife, Zach and Blanche, who live on the property year-round, but they're in a separate cabin, so you'll have your privacy. I've already told them you're coming, so they'll have everything ready for you. If you get bored, you can hop a ferry or seaplane to Vancouver or Victoria, but I doubt that you will."

Quinn wasn't so sure. Wasn't one man's paradise another man's hell? He drank his coffee in silence.

Paul studied him for a moment, hesitating before asking his next question. "Are you going to call Gina before you go? Let her know where you're going?"

"No."

"She'll ask, you know."

"She can ask all she wants, but my plans for the next few weeks don't include Gina Manzoni."

"What will I tell her then?"

"Tell her whatever you want. She's your star, Paul. You'll think of something. Just do me a favor. Leave me out of it."

The ferry bumped itself into place at the Vesuvius Bay dock, and Quinn returned to his Range Rover. He took another quick look at the map Paul had drawn for him before driving off the ferry.

Although he was grateful for the use of the house, he was concerned about his ability to enjoy the solitude. And all Paul's talk about peaceful made him edgy. He preferred action. *Stow it, Ramsay,* he told himself. *You're here to think about an offer on your company in the eight figures.* He smiled wryly. That should be action enough for any man.

He spotted Dogwood Lane and turned left. Paul's house number was carved into a piece of driftwood that marked the entrance to a long driveway shadowed by tall cedars. He turned in and saw the caretaker cottage to his immediate left.

When he knocked on the door, he was greeted by a tiny woman with long brown hair and a big smile. He introduced himself, and she extended her hand.

"I'm Blanche Morgan. We've been expecting you." She turned her head. "Zach, he's here."

Zach's smile was equally friendly as he shook Quinn's hand. "Carry on down the driveway a bit, Mr. Ramsay, and you'll see the house. I'll get the key and be right behind you."

Zach arrived at the house a minute or two behind Quinn, who was already starting to unload the car. He was taking out two mountain bikes when Zach arrived carrying a plastic container.

"Blanche thought you might like a snack. It's a bit of stew and a couple of buns. If you've eaten, she says you can save it for tomorrow." Zach opened the door and headed for the kitchen. He put the container down and helped Quinn with his luggage. That done, he turned to go.

"If there's anything you need or want to know about the island, Mr. Ramsay, let me know. I was born here. There shouldn't be too many questions I can't answer. Paul said to make sure you were comfortable, and Blanche and I intend to do just that."

"Thanks. But if you really want me to be comfortable, call me Quinn."

Zach looked relieved. "Quinn it is. I'm away then. The phone number for our place is tacked up on the fridge if you need anything."

Quinn followed him to the door and watched him

disappear behind the row of cedars. He stowed his luggage in the spacious master bedroom, gave silent thanks for the king-sized bed, and walked through the rest of the house. As with his own home in Malibu, its focus was the waterfront. A wall of glass framed the narrow channel of water separating tiny Salt Spring from its large neighbor, Vancouver Island. Unlike the wide sandy beach at Malibu, here the shoreline was rocky, defining itself in craggy, misshapen stone beyond a tall, twisted arbutus.

He opened a sliding glass panel and stepped onto the deck overlooking the pool and then the ocean. The air was cool and fresh against his tanned face as he watched the slow sinking of the sun. So this was Paul's jewel. Not bad. Not bad at all. For the first time, he started to look forward to the pure uneventfulness of the coming weeks.

"Em, will you watch the store while I run to the post office?"

"Sure. Get me some stamps while you're there?" Emily put her book down and popped open her till while Grace propped the door open between the two shops. She walked toward Emily's counter.

"What a fabulous day!"

Emily raised her head from the till and looked out the window. "It really is, isn't it? I think May on Salt Spring is the best month of the year."

"Why don't we lock up at twelve and have lunch in the park? What do you say?"

"I don't know." Emily was tempted, but she did have those accounts payable to take care of.

"Come on. In another month neither of us will be able to play hooky. The tourists, bless them, will be upon us. We'll have to at least pretend to be responsible businesspeople. Come on,'' Grace wheedled.

"Okay. Why not?" Emily handed her a couple of bills for the stamps. As she did, she heard the jangle of the brass bell over Grace's shop door. Grace sighed.

"Wouldn't you know it. I haven't sold a muffin in over an hour, and the minute I plan a quick trip to the post office, the hordes arrive.''

Emily laughed. By leaning over her own bookstore counter, she had a clear view of the cash register in Grace's store. "Hardly the hordes you might like. It's only Mrs. Duncan. You go to the post office. I'll take care of her.''

In seconds, Emily was behind the counter of Milly's Muffins.

"What can I do for you, Mrs. Duncan?'' she said with a smile.

"Give me one of those raspberry ones, dear.'' The elderly lady pointed to a metal rack filled with fresh muffins. "And a cup of tea, please,'' she added before taking a seat at a table near the window.

As Emily heated a muffin and readied Mrs. Duncan's tea, she thought about her play that would be staged by the Salt Spring Theatre Group in four weeks' time. It was called *A Change in Christine*. How had Grace described it again? A wonderfully warm and funny Pygmalion story. She liked that. The cast was well along in rehearsals, and Emily got excited every time she thought about it. They'd looked good last night, terrific in fact, and Granger, the director, was convinced it would be a success. Damned if his enthusiasm wasn't contagious. If it hadn't been for Grace pushing her, she would never have had the courage to submit it.

After Grace reminded her for about the thousandth time that there was no point in writing plays if nobody ever saw them, she'd taken a deep breath and sent it in. She'd been terrified of rejection—rejection that, this time, didn't come. She dared and won. It was a whole new experience. *Maybe,* she thought, *it was a turning point.* On that positive note, she turned her attention to Mrs. Duncan.

"Here you are." She placed the tea and muffin on the tiny round table. "Anything else?"

"No, thank you, dear." The elderly woman added sugar to her tea and asked, "Have the new romance novels arrived yet?"

"Not yet. I expect them next week sometime. Do you want me to call you?"

"Would you, dear? That would be very nice."

Emily smiled and nodded.

Mrs. Duncan was over seventy and a longtime customer of Welland Books. Every month, without fail, she bought six romance novels. In the summer months, when the island bulged with tourists, Emily put copies aside for her. She didn't want to disappoint her even though she didn't share her belief in the romantic.

Romance, Emily believed, was for more adventuresome people. Her own three-year relationship with Bill Davis after high school surely didn't qualify. That was seven years ago. She'd been twenty when it ended, and she would be twenty-eight in a few months. Her throat constricted as she repeated—*seven years. There had been no one since. So what? Quit feeling sorry for yourself,* she chided. *You've got a good life and treasured friends. Don't get greedy.*

Good thing I wasn't around when old Noah was filling his ark, she thought, a rueful smile playing across her lips. Instantly her visual imagination, her playwright vision, she called it, kicked in with an image of herself standing at the ramp to the ark patiently waiting for Noah to find her mate. As he tried, it kept raining and the water kept rising until finally Noah said to her, "Sorry, Em, old girl. Gotta go. There doesn't seem to be anyone out there for you. Too bad."

The image broke when Larry Enderby rattled through the door, all denim, belt, and keys. He would be disappointed Grace wasn't here, she thought. Emily put her head down and wiped the counter, careful to avoid his eyes when he spoke to her. He made her nervous. Men made her nervous.

"Hi, Emily. Did Grace make any of those banana-raisin ones? You know, the ones she made last week."

Emily scanned the muffin racks and found what he wanted. "How many?" she asked, keeping her back to him.

"Two. Oh, and two coffees to go." He fished into his tight jeans for change.

Emily handed him his muffins and coffee but missed his friendly smile. She'd already lowered her eyes.

"Thanks. Tell Grace to keep making these. They're great."

As Larry went out, Grace came in.

"Hi, Larry. Bye Larry," she said as they passed each other in the door and exchanged grins. She looked across the tiny shop at Emily. "See, what did I tell you? Hordes! Hi, Mrs. Duncan, how are you today? Is that a new hat? It's great."

Emily smiled as her friend handed her the stamps and change. She wished she could be as easy around people as Grace. Why couldn't she banter and tease, make small talk? Why did people make her freeze up and choke on her words? Oh, she was better, perfectly fine with people she knew well or in her store behind her counter. But why couldn't she toss a few bright words Larry's way? *Because he was a man, that's why,* she told herself honestly. The people who made her panic the most were invariably male. *Oh well*, she sighed, *we can't all be social butterflies with a quip a minute*. She headed for her shop, stopping for a moment at the sound of Grace's voice.

"See you at twelve, Em. Do you want a muffin today?"

"Good idea, considering that I forgot my lunch. How about one of those strawberry ones?"

"You got it."

Emily owned Welland Books and half of Milly's Muffins. It was Emily who encouraged Grace to make her living from her talents as a baker, and when the shop next door to hers became available, the two women seized the opportunity. Emily supplied the money from part of the inheritance her uncle left her, and Grace provided the skill and labor. The adjoining door was a bonus that allowed each of them the freedom to leave their shops for short periods while the other covered. It worked beautifully. Emily was delighted to have her sparkling friend so close by. They were good for each other. Grace's exuberance served to drag Emily from her shell now and then.

At twelve-fifteen the two women sat at a picnic table watching the boats in Ganges Harbour. All light and blue shine, the breeze-tossed ocean glinted and rolled under the May sun. Emily was glad she came. She loved her bookstore, but it did feel a bit gloomy on days like today, and this was not a day for gloom. She munched silently on her muffin.

"Larry asked me to go to Victoria with him this Sunday. Do you think I should go?" Grace asked, pulling a strip of shredded lettuce from her sandwich.

"Heavens, why ask me?"

"I was wondering what you thought of him, that's all. I get the impression you don't like him much."

"I like him well enough. He's . . . nice."

"Nice! You think everybody's nice. Nice is nothing. Nice is boring."

Emily watched Grace pull another piece of lettuce from her sandwich. "What are you doing to that poor thing?" She pointed to the wrecked sandwich. "And what's the matter with being nice?"

"Nothing I guess, but sometimes don't you want something or someone who's more than just nice? How about exciting, thrilling, titillating—"

"Titillating?" Emily echoed, then giggled.

"Stimulating, provocative, arousing—" Grace carried on unperturbed. She was on a roll.

Emily held up a hand, still laughing. "Enough already. You might as well look for Xanadu."

Grace gave her a vacant look.

"Coleridge?" Emily prompted with a widening grin.

"I hate it when you do that!"

"Do what?"

"Quote some obscure, *very dead* person." Grace said, making no effort to hide her exasperation.

"Sorry. Just making the point that you might as well search for a mythical Xanadu as look for 'exciting, thrilling, or arousing' on Salt Spring. All are pure fantasy. And titillating? Not a chance."

"So what's wrong with fantasy?"

Emily was taking a bite from her muffin. Grace didn't give her time to swallow and answer before she went on.

"The trouble with you, Em, is you're too easily satisfied. You've made an art of contentment . . . of placidity. As for me, there are times this island gets to me. It's such a small piece of the world."

Small and safe, Emily thought to herself, denying her own midnight dreams of exotic countries and wild adventures. She knew they weren't for her. Given the chance, she would only freeze up and panic. Even if she could leave here, she knew she would always come back. It was home. But she wasn't sure about being called placid. She didn't feel that way.

When Emily didn't answer, Grace probed again. "Don't you ever want to go anywhere else? Wouldn't you like to meet a fantastic man, maybe travel, live in other places?"

Emily didn't answer. Her interest was caught by a cycler coming toward them on the waterfront walkway. She couldn't make him out clearly, but she knew he wasn't local. He stopped a few feet away and got off his bike. For a moment he glanced their way, and a brief, friendly smile flashed across his face before he turned away to prop up his bike.

Emily shut her eyes tight and opened them again, convinced he wasn't real. Until this minute, if you would have asked her if men like this even existed, she would have said no, not without the magic of film and camera work. Never, never in the flesh. But there he was. She couldn't take her eyes off him. A breeze tossed the ends of his dark, wavy hair, oddly sun bleached in the front. He was deeply tanned, she noticed, and aviator-style sunglasses hid his eyes. An early tourist, she decided. No one here was that bronzed at this time of year. She wondered what color his eyes were behind those shadowy lenses. Finally, Grace's voice seeped through.

"Talk about arousing! Is he incredible or what?" Emily wasn't the only one who noticed. Grace's tone was positively reverential. "Em, are you looking?"

Emily looked away. They were gawking like a pair

of open-mouthed adolescents. When she pulled her eyes from his long, muscular body, it was as if she disconnected herself from a dream. She felt strangely sad.

"Look, he's coming this way. He is. He really is."

Emily's eyes flew to the stranger. He was moving toward them. The bile of panic rose in her throat, as her eyes lowered to fix on her pale hands.

"Excuse me? Can you give an island newcomer some direction?" The cycler gave the two women a friendly smile.

"Glad to," Grace answered. Emily was sure even her voice cracked a little. "You can't be lost. The island isn't big enough to do that. Not unless you work at it." She teased.

"No, I'm not lost—yet. Close to it though. I'm looking for—" he glanced down at a crumpled map of the island, "Beddis Road. Which, if I read this map correctly, will lead me to Beddis Beach Park. Right?"

"Right. Just head up there," Grace pointed to a road behind them, "to Fulford-Ganges Road. Beddis is up that road a bit on your left. If you watch for it, you'll see a sign."

"Thanks." He stuffed the map into the pocket of his khaki shorts.

"Where are you from—Vancouver?" Grace found her bearings and was intent on satisfying her curiosity.

"No. California." He glanced at the woman sitting beside the chatty blonde. She appeared determined not to look at him.

"I've always wanted to go there. All that endless sunshine. Emily and I were just talking about that. Well, not California exactly, but other places. I'm Grace Whitby. I run Milly's Muffins . . . over there." Grace pointed to her storefront.

"Quinn Ramsay." He extended his hand. As Grace shook it, she nodded to her right.

"And this is Emily Welland. Em runs the best bookstore on the island."

Again he offered his hand. The brown-haired woman hesitated before extending hers. It was ice cold and trembled in his own. She raised her eyes briefly to his. They were the color of morning rain, gray and silvery. Her lips compressed into a quick, polite smile, before her dark lashes swept down; she didn't speak.

"Nice to meet you, Emily." She pulled her hand back. "Where's your store? I'd like to get a history of the island."

It was Grace who answered. "Right beside Milly's Muffin Shop. You can buy a book and a great muffin at the same time."

"Sounds like a good idea. I might take you up on that. Well, I've got a few miles to cover, so I guess I'd better get going. Thanks for the directions."

Emily lifted her eyes to watch him walk the few steps to his bike. He strode easily on long, well-muscled legs. His shoulders were wide and straight, she noticed, his hips narrow. With fluid movement, he straddled his mountain bike, then bent his head to glance again at the tattered map before stuffing it in the back pocket of his khaki shorts. His every movement enthralled her. It was as though his body was a powerful, graceful instrument under his full and superb control. He emitted energy and vitality like a generator and the potent virility of a proud, confident male.

Emily's heart throbbed in her chest to the point of pain. She could still hear the sound of her name on his lips. To her ears it sounded like a caress. There was another thing. He was familiar to her, and that didn't make sense. No sense at all. Because if she'd ever seen

Quinn Ramsay before, she would never, never have forgotten him. He was not a man you forget.

"Whew! Now that's what I call a hunk." Grace stared after him as he pedaled away; he turned to wave, and she waved back. "Emily, have you lost all five of your senses? You could have at least said hello. You were positively catatonic. I mean, I know you're shy, but you were just this side of rude to the poor man."

"I'm sorry. I don't know what happened. I got nervous, that's all. Besides, what difference does it make?"

"Nervous? Is that what you call it?" The annoyance in Grace's voice changed to concern. "I worry about you, Em. This nervousness—shyness, whatever it is. It's ruining your life. You've got to try harder. Force yourself. Talk to people, for heaven's sake."

"I don't have anything earth shattering to say, Grace. I mean, who'd be interested anyway?"

"Anybody, everybody! You're an interesting person. You've read every book ever written, you're a gifted writer, you're an absolute wonder with a hammer and nails—when I think what you've done to that place of yours—and you have a great sense of humor. Why wouldn't anyone be interested, for Pete's sake? You're talented, pretty, and smart. Not to mention you have an almost photographic memory. What more do you want?"

"A body like Christie Brinkley?" Emily smiled.

"There's nothing wrong with your body."

"Nothing that losing a few pounds wouldn't fix."

"So you're a bit overweight, who isn't? Five or ten pounds is nothing. You could dump it in a walk. Well . . . maybe two walks." Grace smiled.

Emily laughed then. "It's more like fifteen pounds and you know it." She thought about the man on the bike. His lean, strong body was ideal and all coated in a deep California tan. Every ripple yelled fit. *What would it be like*, she thought, *to have a body so perfect? Or to feel it against your own?* The heat that suddenly surged through her caught her off guard. She stood up to hide the blush it caused and started to clear away their garbage. "Maybe it would help if I moved the bookstore away from your muffin shop. Probably half these pounds are your fault. Did you ever think of that?" she teased.

Grace almost snorted in her frustration. "Why is it every woman sees herself as fatter than she actually is? Besides, weight is not the issue here. The thing is you don't seem to care about . . . opening up. Here you are, twenty-seven years old, you don't date anyone, you hardly go out, and you don't seem to want to. You live like a hermit. It's not right. It's like you're trying to disappear, like you're afraid of—I don't know—just afraid."

Emily walked to the garbage can to get rid of their lunch refuse. When she turned back, Grace was staring at her, a question in her friendly hazel eyes. "Is that it, Em? Are you afraid?"

"No. Of course not. So I get silly attacks of nerves. It's nothing dire, Grace. I can handle it, and if it will make you feel better, I'll run after that guy, throw him to the ground, and make mad, passionate love to him. How about that?"

Grace laughed. "He should be so lucky, Em."

TWO

The plan was to spend the day cycling and thinking about the sale of his company. Why, then, did a gray-eyed woman insist on intruding? Wasn't a decision involving millions more important than a woman sitting at a picnic table?

Those eyes. He'd never seen eyes like hers, exotically luminous even in the afternoon sun, made more startling by the intriguing black-rimmed irises. The negative was the expression in them, that of a timid doe. He'd noticed her skin too, creamy and clear, like ivory silk. It would be soft to touch, he was sure of it. But she was pale, definitely not the outdoor type, his type. He wondered why she shrouded herself in that big black sweater. It wasn't cold. And why did she look so fearful? For that matter, why in hell did he care?

He stowed the bike and unlocked the door to the house, automatically heading for the kitchen. He opened the fridge and lowered his head to peer inside. His expression brightened when he saw another of Blanche's plastic containers. *Bless her*, he thought, as he opened it to find a good-sized chicken casserole and home-baked buns. The phone rang as he popped the dish in the oven. It was Paul.

"How you making out up there? Everything okay?"

"More than okay. I can see why you bought this place." Quinn leaned against the kitchen counter and tucked one hand under the other elbow. "A bit quiet for my taste, but it's exactly where I should be right now. How's the movie going?"

"That's why I called. It's a wrap in about three weeks. Would you believe we are finishing up *early—and under budget?* I wonder if you'd mind my company—only for a day or two. I know you planned on being alone, but I'd—"

"Hey, that would be great," Quinn quickly cut in, his pleasure genuine.

"You're sure you don't mind?"

"Mind? Are you kidding? First off, in case you've forgotten, this is *your* place, not mine, and second, I'd welcome the company. It's been three days, and I'm already getting bored with myself."

"Have you come any closer to a decision?"

"No. It's not as easy as I thought. On one hand, I know I should sell. I mean fifteen years is enough time to devote to anything. I'm stale. I need a change. To be trite, the thrill is gone. I guess the problem is I can't see what I'd do with myself without Action Sports in my life."

Paul chuckled. "All that cold, hard cash and you're worrying about what to do? Money opens a lot of doors, my man, haven't you heard?"

"Money isn't the issue. The offer is more than generous. Besides, I already have all the money I need. I guess it's an identity thing."

"You mean, who am I if I'm not president and owner of Action Sports?"

"Yeah. I guess that's it." Quinn wasn't sure he understood it himself. But the past few years were nothing but nonstop work. Forty-eight hours a day, he always said. What in hell did you replace that with?

"I thought you hated publicity."

"I'm not talking about that crap." Quinn frowned. Action Sports was big business. Its blue and yellow logo was a common sight at national and international sports events. He'd worked hard for that kind of visibility. It was good for business. What he hadn't counted on was being discovered by the gossip columns. Publicity was one thing, notoriety was quite another. The tall, handsome, very eligible president of a successful, high-image sporting goods company was grist for their endless mill. He'd hated it—photographers buzzing around his life like disturbed bees, the outrageous lies, and unceasing innuendo. God, if he'd had half the women they reported him with, he'd be dead. A drained but happy man.

"You could always get married."

"What?" Quinn didn't think he'd heard correctly.

"You heard me. Get a wife, have kids. That should keep you busy for the next fifteen years and beyond. In a couple of years you'll be forty. It's worth considering."

"You're kidding me, right? You, Paul Severns, Tinseltown's own homegrown Romeo, telling *me* to get a wife as if women were lined up in a shop window. If it was that easy, you know damned well I'd probably take a dozen—as would you, pal. No, I don't think I can replace my company with a woman—any woman. It's going to take more than that."

"You haven't met the right one, that's all."

"And *you* have?" Quinn laughed into the phone. "Need I remind you of your sterling record, three marriages and three divorces. What's with you today anyway? I thought it was official. You're out of the running. A confirmed and permanent bachelor."

"I am, but I'm not you. You're a softy when it comes to the female sex, admit it. You have been since we were in college. Trouble with you is they come too easy. You need one you have to work at. That'll do it."

"You know what I think. I think you've directed one too many love stories. You're beginning to believe the hype. If there is one thing I'm not looking for right now it's a woman. Got any other—sane—suggestions?" Quinn tried to ignore the pair of gray eyes haunting his denial. Could be Paul was right. When it came to women, maybe he was a bit soft.

"There's always consulting, writing—maybe investing in a hot movie property or two. I'm sure I can find a way to part you from some of those millions. Maybe an artsy little cult film, very avart-garde, that costs ten million to make and grosses three." Paul laughed into the phone. "Seriously, you may want to think about it."

"That's a possibility if you're involved in the project—but no more Italian actresses."

"Once burned, twice shy, huh? Gina feels bad about what happened, Quinn. I don't think she meant for it to go that far."

"Maybe not, but it did," Quinn bristled. "Have you ever had a damned photographer jump out of the closet in your bedroom? A guy put there by the woman you cared for, the woman you were about to make love to. I understand the need for publicity in launching her career, but you have to admit Gina pushed it to the limit. God knows what rag those pictures would have turned up in if I hadn't caught the guy. Someday maybe I'll understand why a woman, actress or not, would want that kind of publicity.''

"Gina is of the mind that any publicity is better than none. She made a mistake.'' Paul hesitated before his next words. "She'd like to talk to you, Quinn.''

"Yeah, well that's not likely to happen in this coming century. Why the hell are you acting as go-between anyway?''

"She is the star of my picture in case you've forgotten. She asked me to speak to you and I have. That, as they say, is that.'' He sounded relieved.

"Good.'' Thinking about Gina Manzoni gave Quinn a headache. It wasn't the first time he'd made a mistake with a woman but never as badly or as painfully as with Gina. He'd thought he was falling in love with her. He shook his head. As it turned out, it was only a severe case of lust. She was the most darkly beautiful and seductive woman he'd ever known. She was also the most manipulative and selfish. "So when are you coming up?'' he asked, anxious to change the subject.

"Toward the end of the month, okay?''

"More than okay. Like I said, I'm looking forward to the company.''

"Looking forward to the distraction is more like it. Trying to figure out what you want from life is damn tough business. If I was any kind of friend, I'd probably stay away and leave you to your agony. But I'm selfish enough to want a couple of days away from this rat race, so I'll see you in a few weeks.''

Quinn laughed. "It's not quite the agony you imagine, Paul. The island is great, and I'm enjoying myself more than I thought I would.''

He hung up the phone, retrieved his dinner from the

oven, and carried it outside to the sun deck. As on most nights since arriving on the island, he would watch the sun go down as he ate. *I may not be any closer to a decision,* he mused, *but I've seen some damn fine sunsets.*

Three hours later, he nursed a cold coffee, thinking about life, his life, without the day-to-day demands of the business. Nothing was clear. The conversation with Paul filtered back. What was it he'd said? About it being damn tough figuring out what you want from life? He was wrong. It wasn't tough at all.

Quinn knew exactly what he wanted. He wanted ambition, enthusiasm, desire. Passion. He needed the fuel that fired him in the early days of Action Sports, before the excitement was wallpapered over with spreadsheets, financial statements, and sales statistics. *I want a fire in my belly. That's what I want.* He swigged some cold coffee and ran the back of his hand over his mouth. The trick was to kindle it.

A bright star caught his eye, and he stared at it, mesmerized by its crystal brilliance. More brilliant by far than its heavenly neighbors. It looked cold up there studded into night's black curtain, but he knew it wasn't. It was white-hot, radiant with energy generated from its own deep center. He wished he was that star.

"Your books are in, Mrs. Duncan, but I haven't unpacked them yet. It'll take only a minute." Emily smiled at her gray-haired customer and headed for the back of her store.

"Okay, dear. I'll browse for a minute or two."

It took Emily only a couple of minutes to split open the boxes and pull out the new titles.

"Here we are. All six of them. Will there be anything else today?'' Emily was back at the cash register ringing up the sale.

"Yes. I think I'll take this new *Persona Magazine*. She's a pretty thing, isn't she?'' Mrs. Duncan pointed to the dark-haired woman on the cover. "Who is she?''

Emily looked at the face.

"Gina Manzoni. A new actress, from Italy, I think. I agree with you though; she is pretty. Beautiful is more like it.'' Emily made a mental note to read the article on her.

After Mrs. Duncan left, she turned her attention back to her book. It was the latest Stephen King novel, and she was completely engrossed in it. The door was open between her store and the muffin shop, and she could hear Grace laughing in response to a male voice. Laughter was a good sound on rainy days like today, she thought. She turned the page and wondered again how the author thought up such macabre plots.

"Must be a good book.''

The deep male tones startled her.

"Oh! . . .'' Her eyes darted upward and widened.

"I'm sorry, did I frighten you?'' Quinn's own dark blue eyes were apologetic.

"No. I, uh, was . . . just . . . uh—'' Emily dropped her eyes and flushed a brilliant, unidentifiable shade of rose.

"I didn't mean to sneak up on you, but the door between the two stores was open, and I thought I'd come in and pick up that book on Salt Spring. The history I mentioned?'' He jogged her memory and smiled.

"Yes. Of course. There are a couple of good ones. I'll get them for you.'' Whatever was scudding around in her chest, it couldn't be her heart. Hearts didn't crash around and bump into things. She took a deep breath to calm herself. This was her store and the man was a customer. She could handle it, but she wished he wouldn't follow her down the aisle. She reached for two books with shaky hands. "One of these might interest you."

She turned toward him and stared directly at his broad chest. Emily stood five feet five inches. She'd never considered herself small—until now. He must be at least ten inches taller than she, she thought. She stuffed the two books into his hands and hurried back to her counter. She needed the barrier between herself and the sizzling male energy he exuded.

Quinn ambled to the cash register looking at the books but thinking about the nervous bookseller. Was this woman like this with everyone, he wondered, or only him? Good thing she didn't run one of his stores. His jock customers would eat her alive. He doubted if she could survive the assertiveness training his new employees underwent before they could be hired permanently.

When he could, he ran the course himself, but the growth of the business allowed less and less time for it. He'd always been gratified when people broke through barriers, those mental and emotional blocks that kept them from living up to their potential. More than once employees told him the course had helped in their personal lives as well. That pleased him. People should be the best they can be, he thought, and he liked to think the training program helped his staff do that.

He put both books on the counter and looked directly at Emily. He wanted to see those gray eyes again, but her head was stubbornly downcast. This frightened woman interested him. Captivated him would be more accurate, he thought.

"These will be fine. I'll take both of them." He

took his wallet from his back pocket. "Do you carry magazines?"

Emily lifted her eyes briefly and nodded toward the front of the store. Then, wonder of wonders, she found her lost voice. "The new *Sports Illustrated* and *Cycle West* are in." Well, it sounded like her voice if you ignored the minor croak.

Quinn looked down at her, surprised. "What makes you think those are the magazines I want?"

"Aren't they?" Emily handed him his change.

"Yes, but how did *you* know that?"

"I, uh, didn't. I . . . guessed."

"Good guess." He made no move to the magazine rack. "Emily?" He spoke her name so softly she wasn't sure she heard right and didn't answer.

"Emily?" he repeated.

"Will there be anything else?" she asked.

He reached across the counter and lifted her chin with two fingers. Emily was stunned into immobility as he raised her eyes to his. His voice was low when he spoke. "Why are you so nervous? Is it me? Do I make you nervous?"

Emily could not mistake the sincerity in his dark blue eyes. Nor could she account for her reaction to him. It was crazy—much worse than normal—and normal could be bad, very bad. She also couldn't lie to those friendly blue eyes. She struggled to steady herself.

"It's not . . . just you. I'm always a bit like this. Sometimes it's worse than others. I sort of—" She stopped, and he pulled his hand back from her chin.

Now only his eyes held her. "Go on. You sort of what?"

"Panic. I kind of panic at times. It passes." *What am I doing*, she moaned to herself, *telling a complete stranger something so stupid? Why should he care for heaven's sake?*

"And I make you feel that way—panicky?"

"A little."

"Why?"

Emily's heavy lashes fluttered down, and she started to lower her head. Quinn stopped her.

"Look at me, Emily. Tell me, why do I make you panic?" Quinn's male ego wanted him to believe it was because she was attracted to him, but he sensed it was more than that. The fear was too strong, too deep. He recognized it from long, long ago. "Tell me," he urged again.

"I'm not sure I can. I don't always know why it happens. Maybe it's because you're so alive . . . so vital." Emily had no idea where those words came from, but the minute she said them, she knew they were true. It was his vitality that scared her. "It's nothing, really," she added quickly.

Quinn considered her strange comment. He didn't know what to make of it or her, but he was curious. More than curious. She was the most fascinating woman he'd met in years.

She wasn't beautiful. Not until you looked into those killer gray eyes. Her long brown hair was thick and, he guessed, soft. She wore it straight, unadorned and tied back loosely with a piece of blue leather. She was wearing the same black sweater she wore in the park when he'd first met her. He suspected she was self-conscious about her body.

He was studying her a bit too intensely, and she was squirming under the directness of his eyes. He hadn't yet responded to her comment.

"Did you want to buy a magazine?" Emily moistened her dry lips and restacked some bookmarkers near the cash register. She knew it was nervous activity, but she couldn't help herself. She wished he would leave.

"No, but I want to see you again."

Emily felt the familiar thudding and pounding in her chest. Air and muscle formed a hard lump in her throat, and she swallowed—hard—to try to shift it.

"How about a bike ride?" he asked. "You can show me your island. Tomorrow? Your store's closed Sunday and Monday. It says so on the door."

"I can't."

"Why not?"

"I, uh, don't ride bikes." She made busywork with papers on the counter.

"You mean you never rode a bike when you were a kid?" He gave her a sideways glance and cocked an eyebrow.

"That was a long time ago."

"You never forget. It'll come back."

"I don't have a bike."

"I do. Two of them. One for me and one for you. It's settled then? I'll pick you up at eleven. Okay?"

"Why are you doing this? Why would you want to go bike riding with me?" She was sincerely mystified.

"I want to, and I always try to get what I want. Don't you?"

Emily didn't answer.

"Eleven o'clock. Here at the store. See you then." With that he picked up his books and left.

Emily sat stunned until the soft bell above her door finished its last chime. *Was she crazy or had she just made a date with the man? She couldn't have! And for a bike ride at that! She'd look stupid and make a complete fool of herself. Well, she wouldn't show up, that was all. He didn't know where she lived. So he'd be angry, so what? She'd tried to say no, hadn't she? He wouldn't listen.* She banged shut the King novel and threw it onto the shelf under her counter. *Who could read?* She stared out at the rain. *She wouldn't show up. That was all there was to it.*

At eleven o'clock the following morning, Emily was standing under the red awning of her store. She wore jeans she fervently wished were one size bigger, an oversized blue cotton sweater, and sneakers. The town was Sunday morning quiet. It was still too early in the season for many tourists, and the threat of rain kept most Sunday strollers at home. She peered up at the sky. It was overcast, but it looked like the rain would hold off. On the outside everything was fine, but inside her nerves spiked and arced like winter lightning.

She felt out of place standing at her own door, and THE DATE, as she now called it, lay before her like a bed of hot coals. She was tense with resolution, as determined to go through with it as she was convinced it would be a disaster. When she saw a Range Rover coming down Lower Ganges Road, she knew it would be him. Rugged car, rugged man. They were perfect for each other.

He pulled the ATV to the curb and jumped out. Coming directly toward her, he took her by the shoulders and gave her a brief kiss on the cheek. When she went rigid under his hands, he seemed not to notice. He smiled.

"Good morning. You ready for this?" He pointed to the two bikes in the Range Rover and pulled her toward the car.

"I don't know," she answered honestly. When Quinn took the bikes out of the car and propped them up, she added, "They look awfully big." Reaching out a hand, she touched the leather seat on one bike.

Emily couldn't take her eyes off them, with their thick tires and wide, flat handlebars. They were both men's bikes with a strong, solid crossbar running their length. She knew they were mountain bikes. There were hundreds of them on the island, but she'd never tried to ride one herself. Emily never did anything too physical. She suspected that Quinn Ramsay seldom did anything else.

"It will be fun. I promise," he said.

"Right. Unlimited fun. Just what I need." Her tone was dry as she warily eyed the big bikes.

"Emily Welland, were you being sarcastic?"

She blushed and didn't answer.

"I thought we'd ride around town first. It's quiet here and flat. When you get used to the bike, we'll head out." Quinn knew she was nervous, and he was intent on reassuring her.

"Head out? Where exactly?"

"Toward the beach I went to the first day I met you, if you think you can handle it." He saw her stiffen and grinned. *The lady rises to a challenge,* he thought. He liked that.

"I can handle it," she replied.

"I never doubted it." He tilted the bike toward her and smiled. "This is your bike. I already lowered the seat, but if it's not okay, I can lower it more. Let's go over to that empty parking lot." He pointed across the road from the store. "You can give it a try and see how much you remember. Okay?"

Emily gripped the handlebars and walked the bike across the street. It felt like ten tons of twisted steel, nothing at all like the old two-wheeler she'd had when she was ten. When they reached the parking lot, she studied the bike for a moment, then without thinking about it, moved it forward and put her left foot on the pedal. She was about to swing her right foot up and over the seat, but when she estimated the height of it, she reconsidered. Instead she tilted the bike toward her and lifted her leg carefully to the other side. Now straddling the brute, she put her foot on the right pedal and pushed off. So far, so good.

Quinn sat on his own bike with his arms crossed over his chest and watched her. Her concentration was palpable. Other than the front wheel wobbling when she made her corners, she was doing fine.

Just then Emily's front tire hit a rock, and it threw her off course. When she tried to steady the front wheel, she forgot to brake and gained too much speed. She was desperate to stop, and the only way she could think to do it was to put her feet on the ground. She landed on the crossbar—hard. Tears came to her eyes as she tried to get her breath, and she squeezed the handgrips so ferociously the blood drained from her soft hands.

Quinn winced in sympathy. He knew she'd hurt herself, and he knew there was nothing he could do about it. "You okay?" He watched her gasp for air, then crush her eyelids closed against the tears.

"Fine. Just fine." Emily was straddling the bike and panting painfully. She'd managed not to fall over, but she knew she'd bruised a delicate part of her anatomy. She'd done the same thing as a young girl when she'd tried to ride her brother Martin's bike. It was painful then, and it was more painful now, heightened and colored with major embarrassment. Quinn kept watching her, and she sincerely wished he would find something else to look at.

"Hurts, huh?" he asked.

"Of course, it hurts," she snapped, surprised at her own vehemence.

He nodded and gave her an understanding smile. Damn the man. She didn't want his sympathy. She wanted him to ride off in the sunset and leave her alone.

Why me? she moaned inwardly. *Why didn't I simply fall off the damn thing? And if I have to hurt something, why can't it be a part of my anatomy I can complain about? The whole thing was mortifying. I can hardly sit here and talk about it—with him.* She looked across at Quinn, sitting comfortably on his bike, his long legs clearing the dreaded crossbar with room to spare.

"I don't suppose this ever happened to you?" she asked.

"Nope." He grinned at her. "Everything there is undamaged and in good working order."

Emily's eyes widened in surprise. He was teasing her. "I'm so pleased to hear that," she answered, trying to sound sarcastic and not quite succeeding.

"I thought you might be," he said with a self-satisfied grin on his face.

At a loss for words, Emily turned away, but not before Quinn noticed the tiny smile she tucked into her shoulder. *A sense of humor, too,* he thought. *This lady is full of surprises.*

It was close to four o'clock when they got back to the bookstore, and in the last half hour, rain fell with a vengeance. They were soaked through, but only Emily was physically wrecked and completely exhausted. Quinn looked almost refreshed, as though he'd taken a quick spin around the block. Emily swore he hadn't breathed heavily all day.

She had no idea how many miles they'd covered, but her aching legs put it at approximately the length of the U.S.–Canada border. She thought a minute. Yes, 3,987 miles sounded about right. She rubbed a throbbing thigh. For a person not accustomed to exerting herself, she knew she'd overdone it, but every time Quinn asked her if she was ready to quit, she'd said no. For some nutty reason, she wanted to prove she could handle it. The other crazy thing was she enjoyed herself.

Still, it was a good thing he was so curious about the island. Without those short stops he was always taking to look at a pasture or enjoy the view, she didn't know how she would have coped. When the stops became more frequent as the afternoon progressed, she began to suspect they were more for her benefit than his.

"Are you hungry?" Quinn asked, still comfortably astride his bike.

He was oblivious to the pouring rain and the fact that his T-shirt was clinging to his muscles like plastic wrap. The rain had packed his hair close to his head in tight, sexy curls, while her own hair trailed over her ears and down her back in stringy, wet strands. Life just wasn't fair. With a quick movement she combed her fingers through it and pulled it behind her ears.

"No," she answered a little too quickly. She was famished.

When she got off the bike, she could still feel the imprint of the hard leather seat etched in her buttocks. Without thinking, she tried to rub it away. She stopped when she saw him laughing at her.

"That won't help." He threw one leg easily over his bike seat, got off, and came toward her where she was standing under the bookstore awning. "Let's have a look at those war wounds." He was looking at her knees.

"They're not serious. I'll take care of them when I get home." She stepped back to avoid contact with him.

Along with the aches and pains, she had acquired a scraped knee and a bruised forehead, the result of a tree's being in the wrong place. She'd traveled that road a thousand times in her car and never noticed that blasted maple. It took a mountain bike to find it—head on. The tumble was grand and undignified. She managed to tear her jeans and sweater and lose her leather hair tie. She didn't even want to think about how scruffy she must look. Much like an abandoned alley cat, she guessed. She took another step back as Quinn continued his advance.

"Stand still. I'm not going to bite," he ordered. He knelt down and gently pulled some threads of frayed denim from her scraped knee. A reddish scab had formed and the fabric was glued to it. He looked at it carefully.

"Not life-threatening. You're right, though, you should go home and clean it up. It could use some antiseptic."

He stood then. With a shop door behind her and six feet two inches of male in front of her, Emily was trapped in the doorway. Her throat constricted, and she kept her eyes fixed on his shoulder.

"Have you got any antiseptic at home?" he asked.

She nodded.

"Bandages?"

She nodded again.

"Can I drive you?"

She shook her head.

He took a step back then, and Emily let a long-held breath escape from her tight throat.

"What about dinner? Say about seven?"

"I don't think so."

"Why not?"

"You don't want to have dinner with me." Emily's

statement lay flat and hard between them. She spoke with absolute certainty.

Quinn looked at her for a long time. Then without warning he lowered his head, his blue eyes marking their target.

"What—" she started.

His mouth found hers with the question half formed on her lips. He gave her no time to react, no time to deny him, and no time to mount a defense. He simply took her head in his hands and kissed her, acting as if it were the most natural thing in the world to kiss Emily Welland on the steps of her own store. His lips were rain damp and surprisingly soft, and her own mouth, softened by shock, opened slightly. Somewhere, deep inside, a switch flipped on, a switch that until this moment had been permanently set to off.

His hands moved from her face to her shoulders before he pulled back from her. It wasn't until then she realized her eyes were closed. When had that happened? She popped them open and looked straight into a pair of exasperated blue ones.

"Now, say that again. How I don't want to have dinner with you. Will it be your place, my place, or neutral territory? It's your choice."

His hands stayed on her shoulders. She looked down at them, certain steam must be rising from her wet cotton sweater. She swallowed to find her vocal cords. Not a trace.

"Are we going to play twenty questions again, Emily?" He gave a frustrated sigh. "Okay. My guess is you would be happier having me to your house. You'd feel more comfortable there. Am I right?" Quinn felt her tremble. He hoped he wasn't pushing her too hard, but he stayed with his gut instincts.

She nodded and raised her eyes to his. Her eyes

made him sad, the fear in them overwhelming any other emotion looking for expression there. Where in God's name did it come from?

"Okay. I'll be there at seven. Morningside Road. Right?" At her look of surprise, he added, "Grace told me. Said you practically built it yourself." He stroked her wet hair, then used his index finger to move a soggy strand off her forehead. "And relax, Emily. All you're doing is being kind to a stranger. It doesn't have to be more than that—unless you want it to be. You're the one in charge. You're the one in control. Remember that."

Emily watched him walk away, watched him load the mountain bikes, watched him get behind the wheel. She continued to stare dumbly as he waved and turned the car up the road to Southey Point. When he was out of sight, she wrapped her arms around herself and headed for her car. *I'm the one in charge,* she repeated. *I'm the one in control.* The words were at odds with the anxiety that punctured her confidence as easily as darts did cork.

THREE

Emily sank gratefully into the old claw-footed tub. The soapy water stung her knee, but she didn't care. She would tend it after the bath. In a couple of hours, Quinn was coming to her house. Why he was coming was a mystery, but he was determined. She couldn't understand it. Hadn't she been her usual tongue-tied, backward self all day? The bike ride was bad enough, but at least it hadn't left a lot of time for conversation. Tonight would be different. Looking back on the afternoon, Emily realized how strange it was.

They'd scarcely talked at all. Quinn didn't initiate much conversation, sticking to questions about the island and the Pacific Northwest. He hadn't asked her any personal questions, and she hadn't volunteered any information. *He was bored to death,* she thought. More than once she'd wanted to talk, especially at the beach. She wanted to know about him, where he came from, what he did—everything. But it was too hard. He would think she was prying.

She shivered when she thought of him, here, in her

house, and the familiar lump formed in her throat. She hated it, hated herself, for letting panic and nameless fears rule her life.

After bathing and cleaning her biking wounds, she felt better, more in control. She put on a pale blue cotton skirt and a white sweater, loosely braided her long hair, and applied light makeup. She was doing fine until she touched her mouth with the lipstick. At the memory of his strong, sure male mouth pressed to hers, a knot twisted in her stomach. The hand holding the lipstick stilled, and her eyelids drifted to a close. Her lips were hot and she touched them with her finger; her mouth was dry. She shook her head and took a deep breath, shocked at her physical reaction to a man who wasn't within ten miles of her. She couldn't deny her excitement, even though it was laced with fear.

She went into the kitchen to start dinner. Above the greenhouse window near her sink, there was a needlepoint sampler. A gift from her mother. She glanced up at it.

> Under a shy moon,
> the tender spirit wakes
> dream seeking, unafraid.

She rinsed lettuce for a salad and smiled. It's Quinn who's unafraid, Mom, she thought, not me. But if I try, try hard, maybe . . .

He arrived promptly at seven. Emily heard the dull rumble of the Range Rover and then his steps to her door. Fighting back her anxiety, she wiped her hands on a tea towel and headed for the door, breathing deeply as she went.

"Hi." He smiled down at her, and despite all her efforts, she felt a catch in her throat. He completely filled her doorway. *If only he wasn't so . . . over-powering,* she thought.

He stepped in, and she closed the door behind him, briefly leaning on it for support. He bent to kiss her cheek but managed only a slight graze before Emily pulled back. He was the kissingest man she'd ever met! He grinned at her. I'll be fine, she thought, but not if I get too close to him. He was carrying a bottle of wine, and he smiled as he handed it to her and started to look around.

"This place is great." There was genuine admiration in his voice as he surveyed her living room.

Emily's house was originally a summer place, a tiny cedar beach cottage, part of her inheritance from her dad's brother on his death six years ago. That was when she decided to move from Victoria and make the island her home. She enlarged the house by adding another bedroom, now used as her office and writing room, pushed out the living room wall for more space and added two large skylights. She'd done most of the work herself, using the island's skilled tradesmen only when necessary. The house was done in pine and refinished collectibles from the island.

Morningview, as she called it, was on the shore of Fulford Harbour, and Emily could watch the ferries come and go from Sydney on Vancouver Island, less than an hour away. The passengers often waved to her when they spotted her on the beach.

Quinn shrugged out of his light-tan suede jacket. Wordlessly, Emily took it from him as he continued to look around.

"You did most of this yourself? Incredible."

His praise warmed her. "Some of it, yes. Did you have any trouble finding the house? I suppose I should have asked how good Grace's directions were." She hung his jacket on a brass tree near the door.

"Her directions were fine. Zach and Blanche filled in the blanks when I asked them to point me in the right direction."

"Zach and Blanche Morgan? How do you know them?"

"They're caretaking the place I'm using on Southey Point. They told me you know each other." He turned to look at her then.

So he was staying at Paul Severns' place, she thought. Zach and Blanche were longtime islanders, and everyone knew about the Hollywood director they worked for. He'd bought the finest waterfront home on the island last summer. Was Quinn connected to the movies? Was that why she thought she'd seen him before? No, that wasn't it. It puzzled her.

Quinn sniffed the aroma coming from Emily's kitchen. "Smells good. Chicken, right?"

"Chicken. You do like chicken, don't you?" She started to worry. Maybe she should have had steak. Men always liked steaks. Or maybe . . .

"I like food, period." He grinned. "Chicken will be great. If you have a corkscrew, I'll open the wine."

"I'll get one." Emily moved toward the kitchen, aware of his following her. She rifled a drawer for the corkscrew and gave it to him. Her hand shook slightly. With deft movements, he opened the wine bottle.

"A couple of glasses and we're all set." As he spoke, he spotted them on the top shelf over her head. When he reached for them, his arm brushed over her shoulder. She ducked under it and moved quickly toward the stove.

"This is going to be a long night if you persist in running away from me, Emily."

"I'm not running. I'm, uh, checking the chicken."

He poured the wine and handed her a glass. "You're running," he stated emphatically.

"I am *not* running."

"Okay." He smiled again and raised his glass to hers. "Here's to *not* running and . . . making new friends." He clinked his glass against hers.

"New friends," she repeated, taking a sip of the wine and looking into the darkest blue eyes she'd ever seen.

"Would you like to go on a hike tomorrow?" he asked.

"A hike? We haven't gotten through dinner yet."

"What's dinner got to do with it? Zach told me there's a good six-mile hike near here. Ruckle Park, I think he said. It's not supposed to be too difficult, and he says the whole trail has great ocean views. Are you game?" Quinn was looking at her over his wine glass.

When Emily didn't answer, he left the question in his eyes and said, "Okay. We'll—how did you put it?—*get through* dinner first. Then, shy Emily, I'll ask you again."

"Why don't you go sit down. The chicken is ready."

"Can I help?"

"No. I can manage, thanks." If he didn't move out of the kitchen soon, she would faint from lack of air. Maybe she should open a window.

"All right. Any chair?"

"Whichever is the most comfortable." Emily turned back to the oven. She was taking the chicken from the oven when there was a rap on the door. She looked at Quinn and at the roasting pan in her hands.

"I'll get it," he offered.

"Thanks. It's probably James."

"James?" Quinn felt irrational irritation that her caller was of the male sex.

He opened the door and looked into a pair of eyes as blue as his own and almost at the same height. The boy couldn't have been more than an inch shorter than he was. Seventeen or so, he guessed.

"Hi. I'm Quinn," he said, offering his hand. The boy looked at the outstretched hand, then back at Quinn's face as if trying to sort something out.

"Hello, James." Emily came up from behind. At the sight of her, the boy smiled.

"Hi, Emmi. I brought Bailly back. I gave him lots of walks just like you asked me to. He was a really good dog, too." Only then did Quinn notice the large dog beside the boy, tail moving like a gyro at the sight of Emily. It was a breed he didn't recognize.

Emily smiled at the teenager and took the leash from his outstretched hand. It was the first time Quinn had seen her smile, and it was what he knew it would be, soft, warm, and penetrating. He would like it, he thought, if she would smile at him like that. As Bailly and Emily had a cuddly reunion, he looked back at the boy. James was openly studying him.

"Who's he, Emmi?" He pointed at Quinn.

"A new . . . uh, friend, James." She turned her gray eyes to Quinn. "Quinn, this is James, my neighbor and one of my very, *very* best friends."

"And Bailly's," the boy added proudly.

"Oh, yes. Bailly's specially good friend," she added with a deepened smile.

Again Quinn offered his hand, and this time the tall boy took it and gave it a quick, awkward shake. "Nice to meet you," he said carefully, then immediately turned his attention back to Emily. "Want me to take him tomorrow, Emmi? Mom says it's your day off. She said you might want to shop or something. She said it would be okay.'' The boy looked hopefully down at Emily.

"I don't know, James. I was planning to stay home tomorrow.'' Quinn fixed his eyes on her. "But, uh, I might be going out. Can I call you?''

James's slow gaze considered this. "Okay. You call me. But not too late,'' he instructed.

"Not too late,'' she agreed. "And thank you, James. Bailly always has a good time with you.''

With that the boy was gone and Bailly was giving Emily's "new friend'' a thorough investigative sniff.

"What kind of dog is he?'' Quinn studied him and noticed the line of hair growing backward along the dog's spine, ending in two small whirlpools of fur near his shoulders.

"A Rhodesian Ridgeback. Don't worry about him. Mostly he just lies around.'' Emily stroked the dog's velvety head and gently tugged an ear. "You're a world-class sleeper, aren't you, boy?''

Good thing, Quinn thought, as he watched him head to the fireplace and stretch out. *He must weight an easy eighty pounds.*

Emily turned to her curious guest.

"Dinner's ready. Why don't you go back and sit down? I doubt we'll be interrupted again. I'll be only a minute.'' She headed back to the kitchen, and Quinn followed her to retrieve the wine before taking his seat.

"Who was that?'' he asked as she sat down opposite him at the small table.

"James? He lives next door with his mother. As you probably guessed, he dog-sits for me. Looks after Bailly, takes him for walks. He's a great kid.''

Quinn considered his next words. "He's not quite normal, is he?''

"No. He's mentally challenged."

"From birth?"

"No. He was brain damaged in the car accident that killed his father. James was two years old. Until then he was a happy, whole baby with a normal life ahead of him."

"Damn. That's terrible."

Emily's eyes met Quinn's directly, and for a brief moment, they shared the pain and sadness of James's tragedy.

"Yes, it is, but he's come a long way thanks to his mother, Lynn." Quinn's interested gaze and her own special feeling for Lynn and James made it easy for Emily to continue the conversation. "Lynn McDonald was a registered nurse. After the accident, she took all kinds of special training to help her care for her son. She said she didn't want to depend on anyone but herself to do what was best for him. She works with James constantly, and even after all these years, he continues to improve. It's a beautiful example of the power of love. Lynn wants him to be as independent as possible. Right now, she's encouraging him to get involved in some special games for the handicapped. He seems to like it, too."

"What kind of games?" At the mention of sports, Quinn's interest was piqued further.

"Track and field. James is a runner. A good one, his mother says. He's entered in the hundred-meter and the relay, although I think this is one challenge that poor Lynn is finding tough. Like me, she's, uh, never been much for sports."

Quinn smiled then. "Oh, I don't know. You did well today, and bike riding is a sport."

"Today nearly killed me," she finally admitted to both herself and him.

"Maybe so, but you were a trooper." He leaned back in his chair and drank some wine. "Why didn't you quit? We didn't need to go the whole nine yards, you know."

"I don't know." Emily prodded a piece of chicken to the edge of her plate. She was surprised at her lack of appetite, especially after the day's activity. Besides, she'd been more comfortable talking about James and Lynn.

"You're not used to quitting, are you? You have a definite air of tenacity about you. There were times today, when we were going up that hill, I could almost feel it. Not to mention that you were getting a mite red in the face. I thought I might have to carry you and the bike back to Ganges."

Emily started to blush, but when she looked across the table at his teasing grin, she smiled instead. "That bad, huh?"

"Tomorrow we'll take it easier. I promise." God, he loved that gentle smile.

"I didn't say I was going with you tomorrow."

"You haven't said you're not, and we have *gotten through dinner*. Almost."

"Almost," she echoed before retreating into silence—a silence Quinn left undisturbed as they finished their meal. Oddly, the lack of conversation bothered Emily more than it did him. He was easy with silence. It didn't put him on edge as it did most people.

When the meal was over, Emily got up and started to clear the table. "Would you like coffee, dessert? If you sit in the living room, I can bring it there."

"Later on the dessert, thanks. I think I overdid it with the chicken, but I'll have coffee." Quinn picked up his plate and followed her to the kitchen. He could see she was getting tense again. For some unexplainable reason, it was important to him that she not be nervous around him. He cleared more dishes, then moved to the living room, knowing she needed the space.

He was sitting on the sofa, one arm draped over its back, when she came in with the coffee. He watched her pour coffee for both of them, then take a chair across from him near the stone fireplace. She looked edgy and the gentle smile was gone. He wanted it back.

"Emily, do you realize you haven't asked me a single personal question after more than seven hours together. Wouldn't you like to know if I'm an ax murderer wanted in fifty states or maybe a husband who has run out on his wife and five kids? Or are you just not interested?"

"Oh, I am, uh, interested, but I didn't think . . ." Her voice trailed off.

"Didn't think what?"

"I didn't think you'd want to tell *me* anything. I mean, we barely know each other."

"I doubt we ever will unless we ask—and answer—a few questions. That *is* how it works, you know." He noticed her faint accent on the "me" in her question and wondered again why this attractive, accomplished woman was so timid, so unsure of herself. It didn't make any sense.

"Are you?" she asked in a whisper.

"Am I what?"

"Someone's husband?"

"No. I'm not." He grinned. *Now that,* he thought, *was a question with promise. At least she's a little bit interested.* When she fell silent again, he decided to carry the ball.

"In answer to your next question—'What do you do for a living, Quinn?'—I run a chain of sporting goods stores."

"Action Sports!" Emily came close to shouting the words as her eyes shot to his. She could not conceal her shock. "That's who you are. I should have recognized the name, or the face for that matter." She looked up and to the left, one index finger tapping her lower lip, as she strained to draw details from the fuzzy memory. "That's it! Quinn Ramsay of Action Sports recently engaged to Gina Manzoni. A dark, super hot twosome about town." She quoted verbatim from a recent edition of a weekend tabloid and looked at him. Her look was strangely curious as if she were seeing him for the first time.

Quinn frowned. "Right on the first, wrong on the second. I am not, and never was, engaged to Gina Manzoni."

"According to her you are. I read it—a month or two ago." Emily searched her mind for the name of the newspaper, but she read so much of what came in her store, it was impossible to remember. It was her turn to frown. "What are you doing having dinner with *me* if you're engaged to a beautiful, talented woman like her?"

There it was again, that accent on the "me." "I told you. I'm not engaged to Gina Manzoni. Never was and never will be. What you read was a mistake."

"Why would she say you were? I mean, if it wasn't true." Emily was truly puzzled.

"For the answer to that, you'd have to talk to Gina."

"She's on the cover of this month's *Persona Magazine*. Have you seen it?"

"No. I don't read that kind of magazine. Strictly *Sports Illustrated* and *Cycle West*, if you remember." It was Quinn's turn to try to change the subject.

"She's lovely. Is she as beautiful in person as in her pictures?"

Quinn couldn't lie. "Yes. Yes, she is." He could think of a thousand things to talk about, but Gina was not among them. "Now can we change the subject? Or do you want all the gory details of my private life?" He could not keep the irritation from his voice.

To his surprise, his cold tone did not deter the shy Emily. In a flash of insight, he realized she was glad he was involved with someone else. One thing about this lady, she didn't go in for massaging the male ego. His own sense of hurt surprised him.

Quinn was right. From the moment Emily put Quinn and Gina together, she was strangely relieved. Her world righted itself. If he wasn't interested in her, she needn't be afraid. She was certainly no competition for the ravishing Gina Manzoni. She ignored the dull wave of pain gripping her senses and told herself that things were as they should be. She was safe. She also ignored the deepening scowl on Quinn's face when she finally answered his question.

"Suit yourself. Would you like that dessert now?"

"No. Damn it. I don't want dessert. I want to talk."

"I thought we just did that."

"That wasn't talk. That was a rehash of groundless gossip, tabloid trash. I didn't think that kind of crap would follow me all the way up here."

"All the way up here?" Emily repeated. He'd said it as if he was on the edge of an ice floe in the Arctic. "For your enlightenment, Mr. California, we read in Canada, too. That is, when we're not hunkered down in our igloos trying to get through our endless winter."

"I didn't mean it like that, and you know it."

"Maybe not, but it sounded like it," she snapped.

"What I'm trying to say is that I'd like to forget about Gina Manzoni and everything that's been written about us."

"I already have. Do you want dessert or not?"

"No!"

"More coffee, then?"

"No. I don't want any more coffee."

Emily got up and started to clear their cups from the table. Quinn watched her in amazement. Whatever happened to the timid, scared girl he'd spent the day with? It was as though she evaporated, replaced by this coolly distant creature who appeared totally uninterested in him. He was intrigued.

"Can you tell me how we have gone from strained silence to a cold war in one headlong dash?" he asked.

"I don't know what you mean."

"We're fighting, Emily. Or hadn't you noticed?"

"I'm not fighting. You're the one who's fighting. It seems I touched a nerve. If I did, I'm sorry. I guess being away from your fiancée makes you testy." Emily walked to the kitchen.

"I am not testy! Where in hell did you dig up *that* word? And I don't have a fiancée."

"You don't have to yell," Emily said over her shoulder as she started to put the dishes in the dishwasher. She was amazed at her own sense of calm—a calm she pulled around her like a dark, secret cloak. A calm shattered by Quinn's coming up behind her, spinning her to face him, and glaring into her carefully composed face. His own voice was tense and controlled when he spoke.

"Emmi, read my lips. *I am not engaged.* I am not interested in Gina Manzoni. Right now, I'm interested in you—everything and anything about you—and only you. Do you understand that?"

Quinn held her by the shoulders, and he felt the tremor begin, a persistent shaking with the relentless build of an earthquake. The trembling claimed the length of her body. Her eyes were no longer frightened; they were glazed with terror. A sheen of perspiration glistened on her forehead. Quinn had never had a woman react to him this way, and for a moment, he was shot with surprise. His reaction then was physical. He pulled her close to him, using his own body to steady her. "Emmi, Emmi, there's nothing to be afraid of."

Emily knew that wasn't true, and she kept her eyes closed tight and buried her face in his chest. Her fingers twined and knotted in the front of his shirt. Quinn held her and stroked the back of her head, willing his own strength into her. When he felt her start to calm down, he spoke again, his soft words spilling through her hair.

"You have to deal with this, Emily. It doesn't have to be like this. There's no reason for you to be so frightened of me or anyone else. I like you. I want to get closer to you, get to know you. Is that so bad?" He continued to caress the silk of her hair.

Emily worked to settle her breathing. Quinn's words and gentle touch were at once alarming and soothing. She wanted to believe him, wanted to deal with her fears and shyness. She'd lived too long with the paradox within her, strength and dread, courage and cowardice. Inside she *was* strong; she knew that, strong and proud. She was independent, ran a successful business, was blessed with loyal friends. Managing her life wasn't a problem. So far she'd handled its unpredictable offerings wisely and well. Why, oh why, couldn't she beat these panic attacks?

Damn it, she thought she had, thought they were behind her once and for all. All she'd been doing was kidding herself, playing it safe. She hadn't been tested—until Quinn came along and turned over her nice safe rock. She shuddered into his shoulder and sniffed. She'd found out tonight, hadn't she? That ugly life-depleting fear was still in her. So deep she could never exorcise it.

She became aware that she was leaning into Quinn's hard, powerful body, taking from his energy and power. Her breath came easier now, but he continued to hold her. *What a fool I am,* she thought, and pulled away, embarrassment replacing anxiety.

Quinn didn't try to hold her. "You okay?" His hands dropped to his sides. He searched her face.

"I'm okay." She brushed down the front of her blue skirt. "You must think I'm a fool or . . . some kind of basket case." She raised her eyes to his with a touch of defiance. "I'm not, you know."

"I know. You just have a demon or two to get rid of, that's all. We all do at one time or other." His eyes were dark and serious.

"I can't imagine you having a demon. You're too—" She stopped.

Quinn gave her a soft smile. "You have the damnedest habit of not finishing your sentences. Did you know that? Now what were you going to say?"

"I was going to say that you're too big, too confident to have demons," she finished.

"Maybe so, but I wasn't always."

Emily gaped at him, overcome with curiosity. She couldn't imagine what kind of demon this vital, confident man would have. She wanted to ask but hesitated.

Quinn saw the interest in her face and went on. "I was one of those Johnny-come-lately kids. An only child, born when my mom was approaching fifty. My dad was sixty-three. I didn't know it then, but my birth must have been the biggest trauma in their carefully ordered lives. I guess they wanted me." Quinn shrugged. "I mean, here I am in the flesh. But once I was there, I don't think they had a clue what to do with me. What I remember most about growing up was how incredibly quiet it was. It was a very well-organized existence as I recall. Even genteel, in a strange sort of way. The house was full of silence." He stopped, seeming to pull the memory from deep storage.

"Where are you from—originally?" Emily's question was tentative.

"Pasadena. That's in the San Gabriel Valley, home of the Rose Bowl?" He looked for her nod of recognition. When there was none, he went on, "That's a football classic, Emily. It's even televised *way up here*." He grinned. "Anyway, I left Pasadena after my parents died."

He looked at the coffeepot before continuing. "If I'm going to bore you with my dull past, I think I'll need another caffeine jolt. If you want to stay awake, maybe you should have one, too."

Emily poured them both more coffee and followed Quinn back to the living room. She returned to the big chair near the fireplace while Quinn reclaimed the sofa.

"How old were you when your parents died?" Emily prodded.

"I lost my mother when I was fifteen and my father a year later—about a year before I finished high school."

"That must have been painful." Emily's parents lived in Victoria, and her one brother lived in Toronto. They were all happy, healthy, and busy. She couldn't bear the thought of losing any of them. "Where did you live then?"

"With my one and only aunt, my mother's sister, in San Bernardino." Quinn laughed softly. "If I was a surprise to my parents, I was the shock of a lifetime for old Aunt Marion. She'd never married. To have this shy six-foot bean pole arrive on her doorstep must have been more than she could cope with. I've got to hand it to her, though, she did her best for me."

Emily was stuck on his description of himself. "You were a bean pole, a *shy* bean pole?"

"I was until Aunt Marion set about, as she said, 'whipping me into shape.' She fed me enough for ten teenagers and, God bless her, got me into sports. All I wanted to do was hide out in my room, watch television, and avoid members of the opposite sex. That at all costs. Back then girls scared the sh— . . . sorry . . . girls scared me stupid. They still do occasionally." He tossed her an easy smile before going on.

"Anyway, the first athletic thing I ever did was in my last year of high school. It was the hundred-meter dash—the same race James is starting with. I felt like a fool. Most of the other guys had been into sports since they were four years old. The track team as a whole had been together three years. I, on the other hand, was a skeleton that breathed." He laughed aloud thinking about it. "I had grown too fast, had no real body muscle, no developed coordination, not to mention no experience in school sports of any kind. More than that, I had no concept of competition. I was a walking disaster. You know the type. The kid on the bench who never gets called. I suppose the only reason they let me get involved at all was I'd lost both my parents. It had to be a sympathy thing. It sure as hell wasn't skill."

Emily scanned the attractive, self-assured male figure across from her, shook her head, and sipped some coffee. "Hard to imagine you warming a bench."

"Believe it. My entry into sports was a full-blown nightmare, and I hated every minute of it. I was terrified to find myself in a position where I had to perform, where something was expected of me, where everybody was better than me. Up until then, I'd quietly gone my own way. All that was ever asked of me by my parents was that I didn't make waves. The whole idea of competition, winning and losing, was foreign to me. Like I said, I hated it. Not a day went by that I didn't want to quit."

"What stopped you?"

"The track and field coach." Quinn's lips twisted into a wry grin.

"He supported you?"

"He told me I couldn't do it. I couldn't win. He wanted to cut me out of a meet scheduled for the following week. Suddenly, it was critical that I be in that race. Not only be in it—win it. I had to try. I was scared as hell. I had no more real belief in myself than the coach did, but I had to go for it. I knew if I didn't, I'd be losing something a lot more important than the race itself." Quinn leaned back into the sofa, his smile erased by past tensions.

"And did you? Try, I mean."

"I did and I won, too. Not first place but a respectable second. I've done a lot of things since then, but none of them compare to the thrill of winning that silver." Quinn leaned back into the sofa and stared at the empty coffee cup in his hand. "When I look back on those days, I know that was a turning point for me. You might say that was the day I joined the human race. It wasn't all a cakewalk from then on, but it was good to be out of the shadows and shake off some of those old fears."

Emily coughed. "This may sound strange but is—"

"Go ahead," he urged, watching her carefully.

"Is that shy, awkward bean pole of a boy still inside you? Do you *feel* him sometimes, nervous and unsure, trying to pull you back?'' Her gray eyes looked at him now more directly than ever before. He knew his answer was important to her.

"Oh, he's still there all right, and every once in a while, he still tells me to quit, not to try. I just don't listen. If I did, I wouldn't be here talking to you. That boy would never have walked into your bookstore, Emily. He wouldn't have asked you to go on a bike ride, and he wouldn't have kissed you on your doorstep. That would have been a loss, don't you think?''

Emily's eyes locked on his. At his question, she dropped them slowly to his lips, then raised them again to nod her agreement.

Quinn's breath caught momentarily in his throat. He wondered if she realized how seductive that look was. If she was any other woman, he would have reached for her. But she was Emily and he didn't. He stood up instead. "It's getting late. For a man who invited himself to dinner, I think I've overstayed my welcome.''

Emily followed him to the door. There was silence between them, but it was warmer, more companionable now. Some of the tension was gone. She handed him his jacket.

As he pulled it on, he asked. "Are we on for tomorrow? I don't think it's going to rain.''

"Tomorrow?'' she asked vaguely, lost in the image of a skinny, frightened kid running his first race.

"Our hike,'' he prodded. "I wouldn't want those muscles of yours to think they've been abandoned. Say about noon?'' Quinn felt a stir of nervousness in his stomach. He was afraid she would refuse.

"Noon will be fine. Should I make a lunch for us?''

"No. Leave that to me. I'll try to charm Blanche into it.''

Emily had no doubt he'd be successful.

As he turned toward the door, he couldn't resist the urge to touch her. He drew her to him and lightly kissed her forehead. This time the trembling wasn't so bad. Another brief embrace and he was gone. Brief and gentle though he was, he left her with a deep, unknown longing.

FOUR

After Quinn left, Emily put on a sweater and headed for the door, too unsettled to go to bed.

"Want to go for a walk, Bailly?" The click of the door pin and the word "walk" were enough to rouse the sleeping dog. In an instant the happy Ridgeback was standing expectantly at her side, tail spinning on a wriggling back end. She rubbed his velvet ears and smiled. At least she knew how to make Bailly happy.

"C'mon then. Let's go."

The night sky over Fulford Harbour was clear now, marked by a full moon and drifting clouds. Quinn was right; it looked as if there would be no rain tomorrow. Emily headed for the beach in front of her house. Bailly surged ahead, as excited on this walk as he'd been on the thousand before it. She marveled at his enthusiasm. Same beach, same route, same smells, yet he never tired of it.

Emily walked to the shoreline, picked up a stone, and threw it aimlessly into the water. Bailly watched attentively. When he figured out it wasn't a stick and that no game was in the offing, his interest waned, and he headed down the beach a few yards. Emily sat on her thinking log. She'd called it that since her first year in the house. She often came here when she was writing and experienced what she described as a brain stall, a time when her creative juices backed up and stopped flowing. It wasn't a brain stall that brought her here tonight; it was a big, dark, sexy man.

She replayed the evening like a videotape. It kept stopping where he said, "I'm interested in you, Emily, only you." Dare she believe it? Did she want to?

"Hi. Can you stand a bit of company?"

A startled Emily began to rise from her perch on the big log. When she saw who it was, she smiled and sat down again. "Oh, hi, Lynn. What are you doing out here?"

Lynn McDonald joined her on the log. "Same as you, I guess. Getting some air."

The two women lapsed into a compatible silence, listening to the soft lap of the water on the stones of the beach.

"Did you want James to look after Bailly tomorrow?" Lynn asked.

Emily thought about it. She could take Bailly with her tomorrow, but she knew how much James enjoyed him. "Yes, I think so. Tell him to come by at eleven-thirty or so."

"You're going to make me ask, aren't you?"

"Ask what?"

"Come on, Emmi. About the man having dinner at your house. I won't pretend I'm not curious."

"James told you, huh?"

Lynn nodded.

"I hate to disappoint you, but there isn't much to tell. Grace and I met him in town. He came into the store and asked me to go bike riding with him. I went. Nothing of monumental importance or anything.''

"You went bike riding? You don't call that monumental? You, Emily Welland, on a bike?''

Lynn laughed and Emily couldn't help joining in. "I went biking, and I've got the sore tailbone to prove it. If that's not enough for you, tomorrow I'm going on a hike. An easy six miles to hear Quinn tell it.''

"Quinn, huh? Now we get to the interesting part. So tell me, and don't skimp on the details. Obviously he's not a local.''

Emily threw another stone in the water and didn't answer, continuing to stare into the dark, widening ripple.

Lynn snapped two fingers in front of her eyes to reclaim her attention. "Emily, are you with me?'' she chided.

"I'm here.'' She turned to look at the smiling woman sitting beside her on the log, and without warning, her eyes brimmed with tears. "I'm scared, Lynn. No. Not scared. Petrified. He's so bright, so . . . dynamic. So, I don't know . . . worldly, I guess.''

"And that's bad? Sounds to me like he's exactly what you need.''

"What I need? Maybe. But what about him? He needs a twenty-seven-year-old *almost virgin* like he needs a tax audit. You know what I'm like with men, Lynn. I haven't got it. Not enough pheromone or whatever it is that attracts them. Besides, he's way out of my league.''

Lynn stared at her friend, her look a mixture of sympathy and frustration. "You're not still carrying around that psychological baggage, are you? Bill Davis was a mistake. The relationship was wrong for both of you.

What happened wasn't your fault. I don't understand why you can't see that."

"What about Peter? I suppose Peter was a mistake, too."

"Yes. That's exactly what he was. You ricocheted to Peter from Bill too quickly. You didn't care about him, and he didn't care about you. You told me that yourself. What did you expect? Moonlight and roses?"

Emily leaned over and picked up a handful of sand. She let it sift through her fingers and watched its downward fall. The sand dust, catching an edge of moonlight, momentarily gave off a faint gray shine. Her stare became vacant. Would she ever believe what Lynn told her?

"What I don't understand about you, Emily, is your determination to quit. To cut yourself off from life because of a couple of bad experiences years ago. It doesn't make sense, and it doesn't match up with what you are." Lynn's voice filled with concern.

"Maybe, but it's tough to accept that I went with a healthy, red-blooded young man for three years, and he . . . didn't want me. That I couldn't attract him . . . in a physical way." Her smile was weak. "How many young women can make that claim, I wonder? From what I hear, most of them spend their early years fighting off overheated suitors. You might be right about Peter. Maybe he was a kind of test, a test I failed miserably, but I loved Bill, and I thought he loved me. Thought he wanted me."

"First off, about Bill, who says he was healthy and red-blooded? Maybe he wasn't. Did you ever think of that? Anyway, you were, what, seventeen, when you started going with him? You told me yourself you were always incredibly shy—that he was your first and only boyfriend. There's no way you could understand his ambition—or judge his libido for that matter. He chose to become a priest because of his own personal spiritual calling. It wasn't necessarily a rejection of you. Down deep you must know that.''

''But we were engaged. If I'd been more of a . . . woman, he wouldn't—'' Emily's voice stopped when she remembered the night she'd found out about Bill's plans, his vocation, as he called it. A vocation that had been on his mind before he started dating her.

It was a few months before they were to marry. They'd had dinner at her parents' place and gone to a movie. She remembered how tense he was that night, how strained the conversation was. That was odd because they always got along so well. They'd been friends long before they'd started dating seriously. On this night, they left the movie, and instead of going home, Bill drove her to a secluded parking spot near Beaver Lake. He wanted to talk to her, he said.

Emily's face still burned when she thought about his request and how wrong she'd been about it. She'd thought he wanted her, that, like her, he was impatient with the chaste good-night kisses and adolescent petting. As they drove to the lake, she'd been nervous but excited.

Bill did not reach for her as she expected he would. Instead, he leaned back against the car seat and stared out the darkened window. She thought he'd never speak and waited, tense and expectant, anxious to feel his arms and to have his love. He didn't reach for her. Instead, he told her he couldn't marry her; he decided to become a priest. He wanted to be a missionary, he said, and go to Africa. He was twenty years old.

Emily was stunned. She didn't believe him, couldn't believe him. She loved this blond boy. Her whole life was planned around him. She'd pleaded, argued, then begged him to give his decision more time. Finally, shy and frightened, she reached for him. If they could make love, she thought, he'd see what he was giving up. He wouldn't leave her then. She would show him the love of a woman. Isn't that what men wanted? How could he refuse? She remembered every button on that pink blouse. There were exactly seven of them. She'd undone every one in her futile attempt to change his mind.

She remembered his looking at her for a long, painfully strained moment, eyes fixed on her young, too plump breasts. Assessing them, she thought. Then, red-faced, he stayed her fumbling hands. "I don't want this, Emily," he said.

She'd never been so bold, never offered so much, but it wasn't enough. He didn't want her. She was mousy, too fat, her hair was too bushy, she wasn't pretty enough. A month later he left for the seminary, unknowingly destroying a sensitive young woman's self-image in the process.

Lynn's voice broke the memory chain. "I know it's trite, but you have to put it behind you. You were just a kid." Lynn looked at her friend and neighbor so lost in thought. She watched a tight smile crease her face.

"And Peter? I should put Peter behind me, too, right?"

"That's right. Like I said, you bounced into Peter's arms within the month. You made love, probably in a senseless, misguided attempt to prove something, and he never called you again. Two rejections in a row. I admit it's a little hard on the old self-esteem, but I've got news for you, kiddo, it happens to people every day—men and women. Why beat yourself up over it? To let it take over your life to the point of panicking if a man so much as comes near you is crazy. You've let it fester into an unhealthy, unjustified phobia. And another thing. It's weak, and I've never thought of you as weak, Emmi." Lynn stopped to give her a contemplative look.

"You know, I don't think we'd be rehashing this if it wasn't for the man you had to dinner tonight. Am I right?"

Emily started to deny it. "No. I just—"

"Emily!" Lynn's voice was stern.

"Okay. You're right. I guess he has started me thinking again. He said—"

"Go on."

"He said he was interested in me," she stammered. "He kissed me, Lynn. Just—kissed me."

Lynn waited before speaking. She didn't want to say the wrong thing. "I can't resist giving you a piece of advice. It may only be worth what I charge you for it, but I have to tell you. Relax. Enjoy yourself, and don't let a couple of yesterdays ruin all your tomorrows. You're shy, maybe painfully so, but don't let your fear win, Em. With a little courage, you can beat it. I know you can. Will you try?"

Emily nodded. She heard Lynn, agreed with her, but it was Quinn's words that stayed in her mind. Demons. That was how Quinn's words described fear. For the first time, Emily gave her anxiety a face, a nasty, gray face with bloody, beady eyes and twisted, sneering lips. She didn't like to think such a monstrous thing was inside of her. She heard Lynn's soft voice again.

"I've got to go, Em. Enjoy your hike tomorrow, and like I said, relax. I'll tell James about the dog-sitting."

Emily rose from the log along with Lynn.

"I'd better go in, too. It's getting cold. Thanks for listening." Emily hugged her. "I'm lucky to have such a special friend."

"Aren't you, though?" Lynn replied, giving Emily a good squeeze. "Think of all the people out there who are stumbling through life without the benefit of my advice. Must be tough on them. Now if I could find a way to coach James in track and field, I'd have it made."

Emily looked startled for a moment and then asked, "Not going well, huh?"

"It's not my thing, you know?" Lynn shrugged and rolled her eyes.

"I know. Maybe some help will come along." Emily was determined to ask Quinn to help James but didn't want to get Lynn's hopes up—or James's. She would ask first.

"Yeah, maybe. I'd like James to do well. It means a lot to him. He's a persistent young man when he sets his mind to something." Lynn gave Emily a quick kiss on the cheek. "Good night, Emmi. Have a good time tomorrow. That's an order." Lynn waved a stern finger.

Emily watched her walk away. *I am lucky,* she repeated to herself, *to know such good, strong women.* She valued Lynn and Grace as people, confidantes, and friends, although she shared her fears only with Lynn. She sensed Grace would not truly understand. *Two different women,* she thought. *Each important to her in a unique way. Each filling a large part of her life, but not all of it—not by a mile.*

"Bailly, come on, boy. Let's go home. We've got some serious thinking to do."

At quarter to twelve, Emily heard Quinn's Rover pull into the driveway. A cord tensed in her stomach, and she took a deep breath. She turned back to her computer screen, finished the line of dialogue she was working on, quickly typed an idea for the next scene below it, saved her file, and turned off the machine. She was working on a new play, and it was not going well. Awake at six-thirty, she thought she would put in a few hours of writing. She'd put in the hours okay, but she wouldn't call it writing.

She glanced out the window, in time to see Quinn settle on his haunches and rub Bailly's big soft head. He talked to James as he did so. James's reaction surprised her. He wasn't shy, but he was cautious with strangers. Lynn taught him well, she thought, but Emily could see he was warming to Quinn. As she started for the door, Quinn stood up and spoke to James. The boy took off at a run. Then, as quickly as he started, he stopped and turned back to look at Quinn. Head cocked to one side, Quinn watched critically. At the boy's questioning glance, he beckoned him to come back. When he did, Quinn crouched, taking the start position for a race. He lifted one hand and pointed to the position of his feet as he explained something. James watched intently.

Emily joined them but didn't speak. It was a moment or two before the two engrossed athletes noticed her. Quinn saw her first, nodded, and smiled. *He smiles so readily,* she thought, feeling only slightly nervous under his warm, intent gaze.

"Good morning," she said a little too quickly, then centered her attention on James, tousling his hair. "Is this for boys only, or can I watch?" Her eyes lifted to Quinn.

His smile deepened. "We were going over a couple of basics for the hundred-meter. I think James here is a natural runner." He rested a big male hand on the boy's shoulder.

James's face was flushed and excited. "Mr. Ramsay

raced too, Emmi. Did you know that? The same race I'm going in. He said he'd help me. Didn't you, Mr. Ramsay?''

Quinn nodded and gave the boy a wide grin. "Call me Quinn, James. It'll be easier for both of us." He turned to Emily then. "James says the games are in three weeks. I'll be here for at least another five, so it should work out fine. Do you think his mother will mind?''

"Lynn? Mind? She'll be ecstatic. As a matter of fact, I talked to her about the race last night. I was going to ask you if you could help out." Emily eyed him hesitantly.

"Consider it done." Quinn wondered why it made him feel good that she was going to ask him a favor. "Maybe I should meet her, though. How about it, buddy? You want to take me over to your place to meet your mom?" Quinn looked at the excited boy standing next to him.

"You want to go now?" James asked.

"Why not? You don't mind, do you, Emily? I'll only be a minute.''

She shook her head and smiled. "Go ahead. They live just behind that row of trees. I'll wait."

Quinn touched her cheek and smiled. His hand was cool, his touch light. "You'd better," he teased. "I don't intend to hike alone."

Emily watched the pair walk away. James was nearly as tall as Quinn and almost as wide through the shoulders, but he lacked the strength, the fullness of Quinn's manhood. A powerful, undeniable manhood, she thought. As she turned back to the house, her hand fluttered to the warmth of her cheek, a warmth left by Quinn's light caress. What could he possibly see in her?

* * *

"We could have stopped sooner, you know." Quinn's words were accompanied by a knowing grin as he watched Emily trying to stretch and bend the fatigue from her back. "Are you tired?"

"I'm fine. One hundred percent," she said bravely.

Quinn cocked his head and studied her. "One hundred percent?" he repeated dubiously.

She smiled. "Well, maybe . . . sixty-five percent. But that's a pass, right?"

"Definitely a pass," he agreed and reached for his backpack.

Quinn spread a blanket on the dry grass. They were in Ruckle Park, just above a tiny cove lined with arbutus and sky-hugging Douglas firs. The beach below was marked by outcroppings of rock and a strip of sand left wet and swollen by the retreating tide. The sun shone fully now, and the grass was bright and warm.

Emily smoothed the end of the blanket and eased her beaten body wearily to its surface. Maybe she hadn't passed after all. Her legs, not fully recovered from the bike ride, were screaming at her unfair treatment. She smiled ruefully. *I guess going from zero to a total of seven hours of exercise is pushing my luck,* she thought, *but, dammit, I should be able to keep up.* She envied Quinn, who could walk comfortably for hours, and vowed never to get so out of shape again.

"Can I help?" she asked when she noticed Quinn rifling around in his pack for their lunch.

"No. It's okay. Lean back and relax."

She was delighted to follow his instructions, grateful to lie back and rest her exhausted limbs. She closed her eyes against the sun as a woozy sense of fatigue slackened her muscles, making her body feel heavy and lethargic.

Quinn was digging into his backpack, spreading their lunch out on the blanket. "I think I've got everything. Chicken, salad, and—" He dug deeper. "Juice. I'm starved. What about you?"

When she didn't answer, he turned to look at her. His glance turned to scrutiny. She looked so relaxed lying there with her eyes closed, mouth loose. He watched her tongue move over the pale fullness of her bottom lip, moistening it, as she took a deep, satisfied breath. Her hands were above her head. For the first time since they'd met, he thought, she looked open, unfolded like a flower reacting to the power of the sun.

"Vulnerable" was the next word that jumped to his mind. Emily had been on his mind since last night. He remembered how hard it was to stop with that kiss on her forehead. He knew he wanted her. That was easy to figure out. His need was obvious, but what was her need? Lover or friend?

He brushed a light hand across her cheek, and surprisingly, she didn't jump at his touch. He stroked the same hand across her forehead, shifting a tendril of hair and admiring the satin of her skin. Her eyes opened, and she looked deep into the blueness of his. There was a question in them, and she tensed.

"It's okay," he soothed, running the back of his hand slowly down her cheek, then dropping it to the shadow on her neck. He rested his thumb lightly on the pulse of her throat. He felt her swallow—hard—and watched her close her eyes. Quinn could feel her tenseness turn to rigidity. Still she didn't push him away. *Was this a test?* he thought *And, if so, was it a test of him or her?* He moved his hand across her shoulder and bent his head to the hollow of her throat. His lips were warm, moist, his breath a gentle whisper against the taut cords of her neck. He fought to keep his hands on safe territory, determined not to frighten her.

Emily lay paralyzed. When he first touched her, she beat back her instinctive urge to jump and run. She didn't want to run from Quinn; she wanted to trust him. She'd looked to his eyes for reassurance, found it, and closed her own. When his lips moved from the base of her neck to below her ear, she rolled her head to expose the contour of her throat and felt the quick inhalation of his breath in response. A swell of heat moved through her, a slow, creeping tide lapping at and eroding her restraint, gently, insistently. She relaxed more when Quinn untied her hair and ran his fingers through it. He lifted it from her nape, kissing her first behind her ear, then below it. His hands tightened on her shoulders, and he lifted his head. Emily's neck burned along the path taken by his lips, and her breathing was short. When she looked at him, it was with eyes bedazzled by the emotions he stirred in her.

"I think I'd like to kiss you, shy Emily. I think I'd like that very much." There was no smile in Quinn's eyes, only an odd intensity, a male ardor unknown to her. His pupils were dark with it, dark and hot. He brushed his lips over hers. Not a kiss, a promise.

"Would you like that?" He toyed with a strand of her hair.

She didn't speak, afraid the sound of her voice would break the fragile thread of magic between them.

His hand rested lightly on her shoulder, where it rose to meet the soft curve of her neck. When she made no sound, he slid his fingers under the neck of her cotton T-shirt, stretching stitches to expose more shoulder, more skin. He bent his head and tasted the newly visible flesh. The rasp of his tongue, its moist roughness on her skin, confused, agitated, then excited her. She waited for the fear, the crash of panic. One hand crept to the edge of the blanket and clutched the long, cool grass. Her other was crushed under his thigh. The fear hovered, waiting. Again she heard his voice in her ear.

"Can I kiss you, Emmi? Do you want that?" His question was urgent now.

"Yes." The word was the barest of whispers as she shifted toward him, watching mesmerized as his mouth slanted over hers. Her heart raced, her breath stopped, and the world receded as she took a step across the threshold of her own terror.

Emily poured seven years of loneliness into the kiss, seven years of denial, giving him both the fire and pain of it. The depth of sensation stunned her. She wanted to touch and stroke him, pull him closer. He shifted his upper body over her breasts, and they rose against the weight of him. Yet it wasn't enough. When her mouth started to open wider under his, she heard him groan.

With a shock, she realized she was giving him more than a kiss. What would he think of her? How embarrassed he must be. With an effort, she planted her two hands against his hard chest and pushed. Quinn drew back instantly, his eyes the color of midnight. He gasped a bit of air, sighed it out, and gazed down at her. She watched as a slow smile bent his lips. His mouth, she couldn't take her eyes off his mouth. He ran his thumb across her lips.

"If you honestly want me to stop, I'd suggest you not look at me that way. You *do* want me to stop?" he asked.

Emily nodded.

He dipped his head and grazed her kiss-swollen lips with his own, breathing deeply as he did so. "Smart woman. I didn't exactly come prepared to make love with you on a beach, as much as I want to—and God, do I want to.''

He rolled away from her then, lying on his back beside her. To hide his physical need, he bent one knee. It happened so fast it was damned embarrassing. Besides, he was thirty-eight years old. He wasn't used to stopping. For a brief moment he closed his eyes.

Emily worked to calm the heat and wind blowing through her body. She was so lost in her own thoughts, her own lack of control, she almost missed his last words. They came to her as an echo, seconds after the May breeze lifted them away.

"What did you say?" She turned her head to look at him.

Quinn shifted to his side, propped his head on his palm, and looked down at her. "I said you're a smart woman. You are, you know." He moved a stray lock of hair to behind her ear.

"After that."

"You mean the part about not being prepared? I just meant I didn't bring any protection," he said matter-of-factly. He stroked a soft cheek with the back of his hand.

Emily flushed a vivid scalding red and turned her eyes.

"Obviously, that wasn't what you wanted to hear. Let me see," he appeared to think a moment, then added quietly, "I also said I wanted to make love to you."

She didn't think it possible, but her face grew hotter still. Thinking she must show purple by now, she averted her face. Quinn studied her glowing blush.

"I've embarrassed you. I'm sorry."

"No! No, it's not that. I'm just surprised, I guess."

"Surprised? That I want to make love with you?" He was mystified.

After a long pause, she mumbled, "Yes, I am."

"I've had dishonorable designs on you since that first day in the bookstore," he teased.

"You have?" She was incredulous.

He rolled away from her to lie on his back. The long, hard length of him stretched out fully beside her. It was her turn to prop her head up and turn to look at him. He smiled up at her, shading his eyes with one of his large hands.

"You remember that bean pole kid? The one you asked about . . . whether he was still inside, and I said yes he was sometimes. When I look at you, I feel like that kid. You make me hesitate, Emmi. I'm not sure what to do about you." He reached for her then and pulled her across his hard chest. "Got any ideas?" he asked as the line of his mouth curved into a bold, sensuous smile.

She tried to organize her breathing. What was there about this man that made her feel so good? Almost lighthearted—definitely light-headed. Was he a demon slayer? *Her* demon slayer? She lifted her gaze to study his eyes, and like sun breaking through cloud, a smile beamed across her face, a dreamy smile, rooted deep in her heart, surging upward to light her eyes, then curling mysteriously around her mouth.

Quinn watched it cross her face, and the force of it stunned him. The smile poured itself into him, to a place deep and down, a new untouched part of him. And if the heart-stopping smile surprised him, what she did next bewildered him. She sat up and hugged her knees to her breasts, looking much like a fisherman with a full net. She looked back down at him then, still smiling broadly, and he raised himself up to look back, trying to figure out what was going on in that head of hers.

"Thanks, Quinn."

"Thanks?" he echoed, without a shred of understanding.

She ran a tentative index finger down his cheek. "For the silver medal."

When he started to speak, she stopped him by pressing two fingers firmly against his lips.

"Let's not talk any more for a while. You said you were hungry, remember? So why don't we eat Blanche's wonderful lunch?"

FIVE

"Old tub, I don't know what I'd do without you. And to think I came close to replacing you with a shower." The water tucked around her as she lowered her sore, stiff body into the steaming tub. "Ahh!" she murmured. "You're a friend in need." She sank deep, ignoring the too hot water. It didn't matter. Neither did she care that her bones ached to the point of torment. Her sense of wonder, the marvel—the magic—that was Quinn Ramsay filled her mind. What trick of fate brought him into her life? Today, for the first time, she felt like a woman—because of him.

She blew the bubbles away from her breasts and smiled.

She soaped herself and smiled.

She looked at her toes curling over the water faucets at the end of the big tub and smiled.

She would smile even more if Quinn were in the tub with her. The erotic thought burned her flesh, and she submerged herself, head and all, in the soapy water.

She came up—smiling.

*　　*　　*

At three in the morning, Quinn threw on a pair of jeans, snagged some orange juice from the fridge, and walked out on the deck. The night breeze chilled his flesh and he shivered. *Good,* he said to himself when he felt the cold air, *it's exactly what I need.* It was heat that had driven him from bed. Emily was doing things to him. Things he didn't want, didn't need right now. She was burrowing into him—deep—it wouldn't work. It was no good for either of them. He took a long drink of juice and leaned on the sun-deck rail. The juice was unsweetened. His memory of their kiss was anything but.

But it was that sunrise smile of hers that unnerved him, reached inside and twisted his gut like the hand of a spirit. A smile so full of trust it made him ache, and it scared the hell out of him. What was happening here?

He thought of Gina Manzoni. They'd shared some good times, in bed and out, but she'd never affected him as Emily did. She'd never made him feel protective or . . . responsible. Gina looked after herself. When he thought about it, he realized that in the past few years, Gina was typical of the women he'd seen, confident, assertive, and coolly in charge of their lives. He was just some kind of necessary adjunct to their image as they were to his. Just two careers passing in the night. Right now, with Emily on his mind, he couldn't remember any of their faces, not even Gina's. Especially Gina's.

He walked to the edge of the deck, leaned on the rail, and looked over the channel. The surface of the dark water was broken by a yellow moon ribbon, a stream of fragile gold that rippled and shifted with the wind and tide. Emily was like that ribbon of moon, delicate, so incredibly delicate. He could hurt her. That thought chilled him deeper than the cold night air. What the hell was he doing, playing around with her life?

The smart thing to do was leave her alone, get back to thinking about the sale of his business, his future, not a pair of shining gray eyes. He wondered grimly if there was any way of turning back the clock but knew there wasn't. He should have walked into her store that day, bought his book, and left. That's all it would have taken, and that's how it should have been. But no, he had to get involved. Paul was right—he was a damned softy when it came to women. The last thing Emily needed was a love affair with a tourist. And wasn't that all he could offer? In a few weeks, he'd be gone. Back to L.A. He drained his orange juice and went back in the house. *Damn that smile*, he said to himself as he once again punched the pillow.

"What is that sound I hear?" Grace yelled through the open door between the shops. "It can't be singing, can it?"

Emily grinned. "There are those who might shudder at the description, but yes, I'd call it singing."

Grace leaned in the doorway, an arched brow punctuating her curious expression. "Is it that California man, or your newfound passion for physical fitness that's giving you such a rosy glow?"

"There are no secrets on this little piece of paradise." Emily shook her head good-naturedly. "Lynn and you got together it seems."

Grace nodded. "And you were the number one topic of conversation." She hesitated a moment, then took a step into the bookstore. "We're both happy for you, Em. But you will be careful, won't you?"

"Careful? You're telling me to be careful? I thought

that was exactly what I shouldn't be. Haven't you—
and Lynn—been telling me for years to take a chance,
to quit being so scared? And now that I'm doing it,
you're telling me to make a full stop at an amber
light." Emily laughed then. "You two better make up
your minds. Besides," her tone turned more serious,
"I don't think I want to be careful. Not anymore. And
definitely not about Quinn."

"Yeah, well, I guess I see your point. He is one
incredible sample of manhood. But still . . . he's going
to leave the island. He's a tourist, and tourists don't
stay. I don't want to see you hurt. That's all."

"Maybe it's *because* he's leaving that it feels so
right."

"I don't understand. What are you saying?"

"I'm not sure, but somehow, knowing that he's leaving takes away the fear. I can prepare for it, be ready
for it when it comes. There are no unknowns. That
makes me feel, I don't know . . . less tense, I suppose.
How can I be hurt about him saying good-bye, Grace,
when I know from the beginning that's what he's going
to do?"

"You honestly think that because you anticipate
pain, it will be easier to bear? That's strange logic,
Em."

"Maybe so. But I feel comfortable with it, and I
don't have any unreasonable expectations."

"By 'unreasonable expectations,' you mean be-
lieving someone will love you and want to be with you,
stay with you? God, Em, there's nothing unreasonable
about that."

"I don't believe for a moment I'm the person he will
choose to spend the rest of his life with. I'm not that
naive, despite what you and Lynn think. He's an experienced, sophisticated man who's lived most of his life

on the fast track while I've lived in a country rut. I just thought, maybe, I could let myself . . . go with it for the time he's here."

Grace stared at her friend. She could scarcely believe this was Emily. "Go with it?" she echoed.

"Just being with him makes me feel alive, Grace. It's like I draw power from him. Is that so bad?" Emily turned questioning eyes to her friend.

Grace shook her head. "No. That's not so bad. I don't agree with your thinking on this, and maybe it is time you reached out, took a few risks, but if he takes advantage of you, I'll—" she sputtered.

Emily laughed at her tiny blond friend when she thought about Quinn's big, powerful body. "You'll what? Hire Hulk Hogan to take out a piece of him? Besides, maybe taking advantage of me is exactly what I want him to do. Did you ever think of that?"

Grace couldn't stop the smile. "Emily Welland! You wanton female. I suppose I should pretend shock at that last statement of yours, but I think I'll eat one of my own muffins instead. I always eat when I'm jealous. Want one?"

Emily shook her head. "I think I'll leave the baked goods alone for a while."

"Uh huh—I see. The California man and muffins don't go together. Is that what I'm hearing?"

"That's what you're hearing."

Grace was still smiling as she went through the shared door. Still she managed one last scold. "I'm still telling you to be careful. Hear?"

After Grace left, Emily moved to the front of the store to straighten out the magazine rack. Her eyes fell on the most recent copy of *Persona,* and when she finished her task, she picked it up and carried it back to the counter, pausing long enough to look at Gina's picture on the cover before thumbing through to the article. The dark Italian woman was dazzling. Quickly, Emily turned to the text and scanned the black and white photos that accompanied it.

There were two pictures of Gina and Quinn, one at a premiere and the other walking down Rodeo Drive. There was also one of Quinn by himself. It showed him in running shorts and tank top, his muscles highlighted with the shine of sweat. He was bending over, both hands on his knees, head up. He was smiling. The photograph was obviously taken at the end of a race. She read the caption. "Quinn Ramsay, President of Action Sports, runs and wins for the Heart Fund in Pittsburgh." There was a brief bio under the picture. Actually, it was more a list of his past female conquests, along with the sly implication he'd met his match in the captivating Gina Manzoni. Emily was a critical reader and the article angered her. She knew instinctively that it trivialized him and whatever was between him and Gina. The article did say they were engaged.

Quinn denied that, and she chose to believe him. Besides, it didn't matter. Gina, California, Action Sports, Rodeo Drive, Hollywood premieres—they were his real world. A world he would soon return to. What man wouldn't go back to so glittering a life? She closed the magazine and looked again at the cover photo. Gina Manzoni was a stunner with a traffic-stopping figure. How did men look at such a woman? she wondered. What was reflected in their eyes? She couldn't imagine, but she was certain that Gina Manzoni saw a very different reflection than Emily Welland.

She was pulled from her reverie by the sound of the bell over her door. It was Blanche Morgan.

"Hi, Emily. Great day, huh?" She came to the

counter. "I was wondering if that gardening book has come in yet?"

"Not yet. Sorry. If you're in a hurry for it, I can call and check on it."

"No. It's okay." Blanche moved leisurely toward the freshly straightened magazine rack and picked up a copy of *Gourmet*. "If I can't garden, I might as well cook." She put the magazine on the counter and dug in her purse. "It's kind of nice having someone different to cook for. And that friend of Paul's sure knows how to eat." She smiled then. "But I guess you'd know that. You had him to dinner, didn't you?"

Emily blushed and opened the till. Sometimes Salt Spring was a bit *too* small. What a grapevine. "Yes, I did, and you're right; he does enjoy food." She handed Blanche her change. "And by the way, thanks for the lunch the other day. It was great."

"Glad to do it. Would have made something a bit more exciting if I'd had more time. If you do it again when he gets back, give me a little more notice, and I'll make you a picnic to remember."

"Gets back? I didn't know he was gone."

"Oh? He said he was going to island hop for a few days. Wants to see a bit of the other Gulf Islands. He and his bike. He left this morning for Galiano." Galiano was a neighboring island to Salt Spring about a half-hour ferry ride away.

"Well, he's got good weather for it anyway." Emily covered her disappointment with the innocuous comment and an unconcerned tone. She couldn't account for the strange sense of hurt she felt.

"Yeah. He does that. Thanks, Emily. Give me a call when that book comes in, will you?"

The tinkling bell sounded Blanche's exit and Emily took a deep swallow. He'd left the island without so much as a see you later. She had no right to be, of course, but she was disappointed. The tiniest bit hurt. *Get a grip, Emily,* she told herself. *He doesn't owe you any explanations about his whereabouts.* Opening the new publishers' catalogue on the counter, she tried to concentrate on the fall book offerings. She would see Quinn when he came back . . . wouldn't she? A gnaw of fear nipped and chewed at her faltering spirit. It couldn't be happening again, could it?

The following Sunday afternoon, her phone rang; it was Lynn and she was gushing. Emily pulled her gaze from the computer screen and tried to take in her words.

"I can't thank you enough, Emily. Quinn is exactly what James needs. He's been wonderful. Comes by every day since he got back on Thursday to help him practice. Yesterday he brought him a special pair of running shoes. James refuses to take them off. I've never seen him so excited. Quinn says there's no reason for James not to win his race. Wouldn't that be great? I've been meaning to call for a couple of days, but my folks have been here and we've been so busy, I haven't had time to breathe."

Silence. *He was back and he hadn't even called.* She felt sick.

"Emily? You there?"

"I'm here." *He hadn't even come by the store. It was happening again. It was.*

"Something wrong?"

"No. Nothing. I was at the computer. Overengrossed I guess. I'm happy about James. But you have nothing to thank me for. Quinn and James found each other before I asked. When's the big race anyway?" *He'd been back for four days. Four full days!*

"That's one of the reasons I called. The games are

the same weekend as your play opening, so we won't be there. James is in the hundred-meter on Saturday and the relay on Sunday. We'll have to catch it when we get back. I'm sorry I'll miss opening night. How's it going anyway?''

"Good, I think. I was at rehearsal last night. I think it's going to be okay. The cast is super." Emily marched out the proper response.

"I'm sure it will be better than good."

"I hope so." Emily was having trouble keeping up her end of the conversation. Her mind was a glut of question marks and confused thoughts, all centered on Quinn Ramsay.

"Emily, are you sure you're okay? You sound kind of . . . distant.''

"I'm fine, but I should get back to this damn third act. Talk to you later, okay?''

"Okay, I'll call you tonight. Bye.''

Emily recradled the phone, stood up, and moved to the window. Leaning her forehead against its cool glass, she stared outside but saw nothing. *He'd been back on the island four days,* she repeated. He'd driven right by her place to work with James, deliberately ignoring her, acting as though he'd never kissed her. Once again she'd played the fool, the silly gullible fool. *You're a slow learner, Emily, a very slow learner.*

Feeling an awkward catch in her throat, she reached for her sweater and headed to the beach. She needed to think. There would be no tears, she told herself. She could handle this; she was a big girl now. She'd lived this long without Quinn Ramsay or anyone else; she would go on as before. A couple of kisses didn't change anything. A man like him was too much for her anyway. She could never measure up, be what she should be to keep the attention of a man like that. Gina Manzoni's face filled her vision. That's the kind of woman for him, beautiful, slim, talented.

The kiss, she asked herself, *what about the kiss?* The answer was swift. *So he tested you, tried you out, so what? Just because his mouth on yours tilted your world doesn't mean it did the same to his.* She didn't have it—whatever it was that attracted the male sex. She'd never had it and never would have it. Her mind moved back to the familiar territory that held her own shortcomings. It was comfortable there, secure. Except for the dry burning in her eyes.

Without warning, a ragged smile wound its way across her lips. *If I'm not careful, I'll go down for the third time in a sea of self-pity—and they'll use blotting paper to mark my watery grave.* She grimaced when the image captured and filled her vision. She saw her hand flailing impotently as she started to sink, felt her lungs fill with brine from the white-capped ocean. A piece of flimsy paper was floating nearby; there was writing on it. Just before it broke up and disappeared into the sea's vastness, she read it.

Here lies the loveless Emily, almost
virgin, willing spinster, wilted
wallflower, silent scribbler—felled by
a kiss. She went down without a fight, a
love coward to the end.

Her wry smile returned. *You're nothing if not dramatic, Emily,* she said to herself.

It wasn't self-pity that made Emily snap to a standing position and turn back toward the house. It was the sharp stab of resolution. *I'm no damned coward,* she said to herself. *Maybe he doesn't owe me an explanation, but I damn well want one,* "and I'm damned well going to get one." She couldn't resist saying the last words aloud. She wanted the water to hear.

* * *

When Quinn heard the doorbell, it surprised him. This was the first time he'd heard it since he'd been here. Zach and Blanche, on the rare occasions they came, always knocked. Behind the door was an even greater surprise.

"Emily?" His hand tightened on the doorknob.

She was fighting a panic attack and didn't answer. At the sight of Quinn's startled face, some powerful second thoughts rolled in. It was all she could do to breathe, but she was proud of herself; she wasn't noticeably trembling. Yet. She gave him a grim, determined stare.

He studied her expression a moment before letting out a long breath. "Come in," he said, stepping aside to let her pass.

Emily moved into the house, her right hand forking nervously through her hair, pushing it back behind her ear. When she heard Quinn come up behind her, she spun to look at him with raised chin. The lines of her face were stubborn, unyielding.

"Emily—" he started.

"What exactly are you doing?" she demanded.

"Doing?"

"On this island, on Salt Spring. Why are you here?" These were not the questions she intended to ask, but they were a start.

He didn't answer. She was angry and hurt, he could see that. He decided to play for time. It irritated him to admit it, but maybe he did owe her an explanation. Ignoring her question, he asked, "Have you eaten? I was about to have dinner. I'm on my own tonight. Blanche has forsaken me for a weekend with Zach in Vancouver. If you can handle a steak and a salad, I've got enough."

Emily shook her head in frustration.

He ignored that too and took her elbow to direct her to the sun deck. "Why don't we talk while I cook? How do you like your steak? Let me guess . . . medium. Right?" They were on the deck now, and Quinn dropped his hand from her elbow.

"I told you. I don't want a steak," she said.

"Loosen up and humor me, okay? I'm tired of eating alone. Medium?" he asked again.

Quinn took her stony silence for acceptance.

"Good. Medium it is. We'll talk while we eat." He looked at her and couldn't resist running two cool fingers across the heat of her cheek before moving to the barbecue. "I'm glad you came. I've missed you."

"Missed me!" Emily didn't bother to mask her surprise, and she almost spat out her next question. "If you missed me, why didn't you call, come by—something?" There it was. Out in the open. The minute she said it, she wanted the words back. She was crazy to come here. Where was her pride? Buried under overwhelming curiosity, that's where. The new, improved Emily wanted—*needed*—to know why she was rejected. She could not move forward without knowing. Damn any pride standing in the way of that. She straightened her shoulders and stared at him.

"Why?" she repeated.

"I thought it was the right thing to do." His gaze stayed level with hers while his hands slipped into the back pockets of his jeans.

"The right thing to do?" She stared at him. His answer told her nothing. "I don't understand."

"I like you, Emily. Too damn much." He paused. "And what you don't need is a short-term relationship with a one-time visitor to your island."

"You decided that all by yourself, did you?" Emily

felt heat rising to her face, but it was not the heat of fear; it was the heat of anger. Who was he to decide what was good for her and what was not? What did he know about her needs? "That's a bit arrogant, don't you think? Making decisions for me on the basis of a few hours together."

"Maybe so. But you're just something I didn't plan on. That's all."

"I'm not a 'thing.' In case you haven't noticed, I'm a woman." Her eyes widened in anger.

"I noticed. Believe me, I noticed." Quinn turned to the gas barbecue, put on a couple of potatoes, and closed the lid. This whole conversation was getting out of hand.

"So?" Emily leaned against the cedar railing of the deck, taking balance from the solid feel of the wood.

"So? So, what?" Quinn turned back to look at her, his expression quizzical.

"What are you going to do about it?"

"You lost me. Do about what?"

"About my being a woman. That's what." With that remark, Emily took a quantum leap into unmapped territory. She refused to second guess what she said or why she said it. She was driven only by a sense of crisis. She was convinced now that what was happening, *what would happen*, between her and Quinn was a catalyst, a stepping stone to a fuller, more courageous life.

To say her question stunned him was an understatement. It knocked him out. There was nothing seductive in Emily's tone when she asked it, no come-on, no teasing, not a trace of flirtation. The question was bold, flat, and direct, and accompanied by the steady gaze of her gray eyes, it was the most erotic question he'd ever heard. Quinn had tried all week to lower the temperature of his desire, and now with one look from those rain-colored eyes, he was burning again. What was dangerous about Emily, he decided, was that she had no idea what she did to him.

She stood waiting for his answer. Stymied, he parried with a question of his own.

"What exactly am I expected to do about it? Is there something specific you have in mind?" His eyes locked with hers.

Emily met his gaze without wavering, then turned away. Her fingers gripped the deck rail until her knuckles were a bloodless white. She stared at the ocean and didn't turn back to him when she spoke again.

"Forget it. It was stupid of me to come here. I'm good at that, you know . . . doing stupid things."

"I don't see anything stupid about it. You wanted something and you went after it. There's nothing stupid about that. What was stupid—unforgivable—was my not seeing you again. I did exactly what I tried not to. I hurt you. I should have called. I'm sorry." Quinn's voice was soft, so gentle his words scarcely carried to where she was standing.

Emily turned to face him. "Yes . . . well . . . you don't owe me anything, least of all an apology, but thanks anyway. I think I'd better go."

He took a step toward her to block her path. "Don't go." He placed his big hands on her shoulders and looked down at her. "Stay. Please."

Emily kept her eyes steady when she looked up to him. There was no point acting the scared rabbit at this point. "You want me to stay? Or are you being kind?"

"I want you to stay, and believe me, being kind has nothing to do with it." He brushed his lips across hers and ran his hands down her arms until he clasped her hands. He pulled back then. ''We'll have dinner and then we'll talk. Deal? I think I'd like to answer your questions. Both of them. First, about what I'm doing here on the island, and second, what I'm going to do about the fact that you're a woman. Stay.'' The last word was more demand than request.

The light kiss brought his scent with it, accented with his clean, musky after-shave; she breathed him in. She would stay, she decided, but she would watch for warning flags—and would not, absolutely not, be hurt again. Nor would she be a love coward. With effort she pulled away from his warmth and looked up at him.

''I'll stay,'' she stated firmly.

He smiled and dropped her hands. ''Good. Now, no more talk until I ruin a couple of steaks for us. Agreed?''

She nodded, but without his warm grip, she was tense and self-conscious. ''Can I do anything? Make the salad?''

''Sure. Everything you need is in the kitchen.'' Quinn pointed in the direction of the house with a long-handled lifter.

He watched her walk into the big house, and the smile left his face. He was making a big mistake; he could feel it. Her question hummed in his brain. ''I'm a woman. What are you going to do about it?'' He took a deep breath as he saw her disappear behind the opened fridge door. *I sure as hell know what I'd like to do,* he thought. Feeling unsettled and oddly indecisive, Quinn turned back to the steaks.

During dinner, he worked hard to keep an easy flow of conversation going, drawing her out, encouraging her to relax, and most of all trying to take away the hurt he'd caused. So the steaks were overcooked and the potatoes a mite underdone. It didn't matter. What mattered was Emmi. They talked about the island, California, James, and the forthcoming games. Quinn was enthusiastic about his chances of winning. It pleased him to see the boy try so hard. He liked people who tried hard. For the first time, he heard about Emily's writing, her coming debut as a playwright. When she became uncomfortable talking about herself, she changed the subject. She was good at that, he noticed.

When Quinn told her why he'd come to Salt Spring, about the difficulty of deciding to sell his business, she listened with keen interest, her eyes never leaving his face. He hadn't realized until now how much he'd needed to discuss it with someone.

"To tell the truth, I'm nervous about life after Action Sports. I've been so tied up in the business for so long I don't know where I begin and the stores end. It's like a part of me. On the one hand, I hate to leave it, and on the other, I've got this gut instinct that it's time. Time for a change. Does that sound stupid?" He leaned back in his chair and absently drank some wine.

"That bean pole kid making trouble for you again, huh?" Emily asked gently.

He grinned and nodded. "I guess so." This woman made him feel good, he thought as he looked across at her. Damn good. It was dark now, and her face was lit only by a slant of light coming from the living room. Her long lashes shadowed her cheeks.

"When you decide, you'll do the right thing. But . . ." she stopped, unwilling to give an unsolicited opinion.

He leaned forward and urged her on. "But what? Go on. What were you going to say?"

"I was going to say what seems truly important is that your decision to sell be based more on the future than the past. Not what you're leaving behind so much as what you're moving toward. Maybe if you knew clearly what you wanted to do after Action Sports, the decision would be easier, more comfortable. I guess that sounds kind of muddled,'' she trailed off.

"No. That doesn't sound muddled at all. You're right on the mark. That's exactly what I have been doing, thinking about the past instead of the future.'' He reached across the table and took her hand. "How did you get to be so smart anyway? Or are you a natural student of human nature?'' Quinn was more convinced than ever—this woman was special. He stroked the back of her hand with his thumb. The connection warmed him.

The caress of his thumb did strange things to Emily's vocal cords, so she didn't answer his question. She did lift her eyes to look at him. She could look at him forever, she thought, watching his expression deepen as he continued to stroke her hand. His next words took her breath, and her eyelids fluttered downward.

"How about we move on and talk about the second question?'' There was a trace of tease in his words. "Let's talk about your being a woman and what I'd like to do about it. That was your question, wasn't it?''

Her eyes shot to his. What had she been thinking to ask such a thing, and how could she get out of this?

"You don't have to . . . I didn't mean to . . . Can't we forget it?'' Her nerves, until now calmed by his easy conversation, started to jump and pitch. She tried to withdraw her hand from his, but he held her fast.

"I don't want to forget it. And I don't think you want to either.'' He stood up and pulled her with him. "It's getting cold out here. Let's go in.''

Emily pulled back. "It's not cold.''

"Maybe not to you, but to this recently transplanted Californian, it's cold." He grinned and gave her hand another tug. "Now are we going to stay out here and play tug of war, or are you coming inside?"

SIX

Emily swallowed deep and followed him, all the while ignoring the clacking and clattering of her nerves. He led her to a leather sofa and left her there while he retrieved their wine glasses. That done he sat down, not beside her as she expected, but on the floor, his back resting on the matching love seat across from her, long legs extended across the deep carpet.

"You going to stay up there or come down here with me?"

"I'm fine here." She was perched on the edge of the sofa with the readiness of a jet on a launching pad.

"No, you're not. Come here. I want you close to me." He reached for her hand and pulled her down to the soft carpet. In one easy movement, he placed her squarely in the vee between his legs with her back against the wall of his chest. He wrapped his arms close about her and put his mouth to her ear. "There. That's a lot better, isn't it? Especially since we are about to have an intimate conversation—a very intimate conversation. That's what you want, isn't it, Emily?"

She didn't know what she wanted, but she liked what he was giving her. She nodded agreement, closed her eyes, and laid her head back against his shoulder. His cuddling was delicious. Quinn groaned softly and raised one hand to her neck, nicely exposed by the scooped neckline of her T-shirt.

He lifted her hair from her ear, and his teeth nibbled, then pulled lightly on her earlobe. Until he did that, Emily hadn't known that her earlobe was connected to her stomach, along with an even more sensitive part of her anatomy. Her spinal cord weakened and her head fell sideways. Quinn bit her softly where her neck met her shoulder, and she shifted between his legs to ease the throb between her own.

That shift brought a soft explosion of breath from Quinn's mouth. He pulled his head back and ran his hands down her arms, resting them near her elbows.

"Maybe this wasn't such a good idea after all. If you're going to sit here, you're going to have to sit still or I might do something you're not quite ready for."

"Do you want me to move?"

Again he wrapped his arms around her. "Not on your life. You stay right where you are. I want to hold you."

They fell silent then. The only sound was the wind in the trees and the low muttering of the ocean coming through the open patio doors.

Emily was happy in the silence, all wrapped as she was in Quinn's arms, but it was she who spoke first.

"Quinn?"

"Uh-huh." His hands started moving again, slipping under her arms and down to stroke her jeans-clad legs. When they slipped to her inner thighs, he withdrew them. Damn, she was so open to him, but still he hesitated.

"Tell me, Quinn. Tell me what you want to do with me."

"How about if I show you instead?" He pulled her to him hard and buried his head in the recess of her shoulder. "At the moment I'm not sure I can put words together and make any sense of them." He kissed her throat, quick burning kisses like tiny brands. She knew they would still be there tomorrow, and she ached with the pleasure of them.

"Try." She liked the new lowered timbre of his voice.

"You're a cruel woman to make a man talk when he's practically crippled with need." He pulled his head from her shoulder and leaned back against the leather love seat, then circled his hands loosely at the base of her neck. They lay there unmoving while he took a couple of calming breaths.

"I want to make love with you, Emmi. I've wanted to since that day in the park. I want your body under mine, your breasts filling my hands. I want to touch you, kiss you—taste you," he smiled into her hair, "in all the most sinful places. I want to be inside you . . . feel you hot and wet. I want you to melt for me. . . . You make me burn, shy Emily." He buried his face in her hair, and his voice was thick and untrustworthy when he repeated, "You make me burn."

Quinn's words twisted through her like a rope pulled fast and hard, scorching everything it touched. If he could do this with words, what a glorious blaze his hands and mouth would kindle. She tensed, not with fear, but with anticipation of what would follow. What *must* follow. He went on.

"But more than any of that, I don't want to hurt

you, and I don't want to be dishonest. I can't make a commitment. In a month I'll be gone, and I don't think you need a transient lover. Chances are that I'll never be on this island again.'' His hands left their place at the base of her neck and came to rest on his own extended legs. The movement was not without effort.

Emily snapped to her knees and turned to face him. "But don't you see, that's exactly what I need. I want you, too . . . and I want those feelings. Can you make me feel that way, Quinn? Can you?''

"Do you know what you're saying?" Her fevered reply startled him. Was she asking what he thought she was asking?

"Yes. I know exactly what I'm saying. I'm saying I want to make love with you and I accept the consequences. I *want* to be seduced." Her eyes were steady as she studied Quinn's stunned expression, looking for any trace of rejection.

What she saw in his cocked head and raised eyebrows was the dawning of suspicion. He touched her face gently and watched her eyes carefully when he asked, "Emily, you're not a virgin, are you?" He was prepared to believe it.

She dropped her eyes.

"God! You are, aren't you?"

"No, I'm not. Not exactly."

"Not exactly?"

"I've made love before. So you don't need to worry about deflowering me. If that's what's bothering you."

"Deflowering—? How long ago was this affair, this 'deflowering'?"

Silence.

"Emily, answer me."

"I made love . . . once . . . seven years ago." Scarlet burned her cheeks.

Quinn let out a long breath. The embarrassed look on her face made him want to reach for her and pull her close. He resisted. His next thought was amazement that the male population of the world had blindly passed this woman by. Took too much effort, he suspected. He looked back at her, sensing his silence was causing her pain.

"Why don't you tell me about it?"

Face burning, she hesitated. She couldn't tell this experienced, worldly man about her disastrous juvenile relationships. He'd think her a fool. She glanced up at him and saw his blue eyes riveted to hers. He nodded, urging her on.

"All right." She raised her head and lifted her chin. "I'll tell you, but you have to promise you won't laugh."

"Laugh? Why would I laugh?"

"Because men think women like me are weird. That we're a kind of joke or throwback. Maybe even . . . frigid."

"I think we've already established that you're no expert when it comes to men, Emmi. So maybe you'd better lay off the generalizations. Okay? Now come on. Talk."

Emily did talk, telling him about Bill's becoming a priest and her boomerang tryst with Peter. Even though she made short work of the story, Quinn could feel her uncertainty and the underlying ache that had stayed with her all these years. He shook inwardly when he thought about how she must have felt when he hadn't called— all the old fears emerging to wreak havoc on her fragile self-image. He cursed himself, this time vehemently. He heard her finish.

". . . left me kind of phobic, nervous. I know it's dumb, but it's like I shut down. Until you." Gray eyes met blue. "Somehow you pushed through all that. That's why I want to—" She stopped. She'd said enough.

"Want to have sex with me?" he finished. "What about love? Don't you want that?"

"Of course. But not from you."

"Thanks. Thanks a lot."

Emily blushed furiously. "I didn't mean it the way it sounded. I meant I don't expect a man like you to love me. It wouldn't be . . . natural."

Quinn threw back his head and laughed. "God, woman, you do have a turn of phrase. Not natural? You make me sound like an alien life form."

"You're deliberately misunderstanding me. I was trying to point out how different we are. That's all. I could never be what you need." She fixed somber eyes to his. "Never."

His breath lodged in his throat when her eyes caught his and tugged at his resolve. His next words came without thought. "Never say never, Emily."

At this moment, in this quiet room, Quinn knew anything was possible. Could he love this woman? Was it really so impossible?

He reached for her then. Taking her serious face between his hands, he pulled it to him, his thumbs moving gently over her soft complexion. His mouth hovered over hers as he spoke. "I think it's time you went home, but before you do . . ."

He ran his tongue slowly, evocatively along the crevice of her lips, seeking entry. Emily quivered, and when her lips parted, his tongue entered, teasing, prodding, the stroke of it slow, hot, and sensual. When his tongue moved inward, her soft moan called to him until he claimed her mouth fully, deeply. Her hands, flat against his chest, moved to the muscles of his shoulders, where her fingers curled and bit into them before tangling in his dark hair. She'd thought it couldn't get any better than the kiss on the beach. She was wrong.

The taste, the intimacy of his tongue curling around her own ignited her, and she cried into his mouth, the core of her melting under his hot, demanding lips. She sagged when he pulled back, his hands still holding her face. How strange, she thought, his hands barely moved, yet she was touched, caressed, all over.

Trembling with restraint, he held her from him. His voice was low and husky when he said, "You'd better go, Emily."

"You don't want me then?" He saw agony in her eyes, the certainty of rejection.

"Don't want you? I want you so bad I need a pain killer, but I have to think . . . more important, *you* have to think. You have to be sure." He forced a smile. "Go home, please, before I forget myself. I'll call you tomorrow. I promise."

Emily drove home on autopilot. She could think of nothing except the sensation of Quinn's mouth covering hers. She remembered his dark blue eyes, interested and thoughtful, as she told him things she never believed she could tell a man. She didn't regret her rash decision to confront him tonight. To have experienced that one glorious kiss was reward enough. If she never saw him again . . .

At that thought, Emily felt the familiar stirring of anxiety. She pulled the car to the side of the darkened road and leaned her head on the steering wheel. In a month, he'd be gone. *Remember that*, she told herself. *Don't start to dream the impossible dream. He told you . . . no commitments. Live with it or go back under your rock, woman. He doesn't want your love—*

Emily sat bolt upright and gripped the wheel until her hands ached. *I love him. I do.* Tears burned behind her tightly closed lids. I love him and already it hurts. Grace was right. Anticipating pain doesn't make it hurt less. She shook her head to clear it and reached in the glove compartment for a tissue. It didn't matter. None of it mattered. She would have this month with him. She would risk the hurt. It was worth it. And when he left, she would paste the memory, like an old yellowed photograph, in the album of her heart. That memory would be worth the price of a few tears. That memory would be worth anything.

The next morning it was raining, a Pacific Northwest downpour, strong and steady. Emily could hear it bouncing off the skylights in her living room. She forced herself to look at the brass clock beside her bed and moaned. Ten to ten. It had to have been six-thirty or so before she'd finally fallen asleep. Feeling much like a sack of wet cement, she dragged herself from bed and headed to the bathroom. *This is not how you expect to feel after a night with the most exciting man you've ever met,* she thought.

A look in the mirror told the bald truth. Her skin matched her eyes perfectly. Not exactly the black death but certainly gray. She ached all over, and her rolling stomach confirmed this was more than from lack of sleep. Grateful it was Monday and the store was closed, she headed back to bed. She would take an aspirin, sleep a while longer, and this plague would pass.

Bailly breathed in her face about an hour later. She opened one eye and looked at him. A dog smile was in his eyes and his tail wagged expectantly. Emily gave him as close to a human smile as she could muster and threw the covers back. The poor beast's bladder must be bursting, she thought, feeling guilty for not letting him out earlier. Grabbing a cotton robe, she followed him to the door.

"You're not going to be pleased, big guy. It's awfully wet out there."

When she opened the door, Bailly looked out and then back to her to see if she would stop the rain. When she shook her head, he sat down in the open doorway, eyeing the dampness with bleak but patient demeanor. If she wouldn't stop it, he would wait it out. Bailly hated to get wet. Emily nudged his rear end with a slipper-clad foot.

"Sorry, fellah, but there's nothing I can do about it. Away you go." Head down, ears back, Bailly obliged, but Emily knew he wouldn't be long.

She went to the kitchen for a couple more aspirins. She still ached all over, and she could feel the start of a headache. It was not going to be a good day. When Bailly came back, she would go back to bed. For the moment, she stretched out on the couch. She was asleep instantly.

"Emily. *Emily.*"

The hand on her shoulder gave a gentle shake and her heavy eyelids opened. She must be dreaming. It couldn't be Quinn standing over her. She blinked again. It *was*.

"What are you doing sleeping on the couch?" he asked.

She sat up and rubbed her eyes. God, what she must look like. Not exactly love in bloom, she was sure of that. She ran her fingers through her sleep-mashed hair and sat up. He smelled outdoorsy and rain fresh and looked like some kind of rain god, if there was such a thing. If there wasn't, she thought, he'd do.

"What are you doing here?" she asked, ignoring his question, looking instead at his wet hair, beaded and glistening with the sky's moisture.

"For a while it looked like this damned deluge was going to stop, so I thought I'd be able to run with James. But by the time I got here, it was pouring again. Besides, it seems he has some kind of flu bug. I thought I'd come by for a cup of coffee. I knocked; I guess you didn't hear me." He gave her an appraising look. "You okay?"

"Other than the fact I ache all over, I'm fine. I guess I have what James has. But I'm well enough to make you a cup of coffee." She started to get up, but he pushed her down.

"I'll make my own. How about you? Can I get you anything?" As he started for the kitchen, she shivered and he glanced back to her. "You really are sick, aren't you? Come on. I'm putting you back in bed." His voice was firm.

He picked her up.

"Bedroom?" he asked, looking at the doors leading from the living room.

She nodded mutely in its general direction.

He carried her to the bed, sat her on its edge, and took off her robe. No man had ever set foot in her bedroom before and certainly none undressed her while she sat still as a stone and let him. It happened so fast, and Quinn was so calm about it, she was stunned into embarrassed acceptance.

The situation was so unbelievable as to be unreal. What was very real was the look Quinn gave her when he saw the sheer nightgown she was wearing. The pearl-gray silk was the color of polished silver. The gown had string straps and a matching lace bodice. It was a birthday gift from Grace. It arrived, Emily remembered, with a toast written on the card, "Here's to getting lucky." After last night with Quinn, it was the only nightgown she'd deemed suitable.

"Shouldn't you be wearing something warmer?" His eyes raked over her very visible form. "That's hardly sickbed attire."

"This will be fine." She dove into bed and yanked the covers to her chin, face scarlet.

He smiled. "You have a wonderful body, you know. There's no need to be ashamed of it."

She stared at him in total disbelief. Damned if he didn't look sincere. She muttered into the pillow.

"What did you say?" He bent his dark head toward her.

"I was asking myself if I'd buy a used car from this man."

He laughed. "You're hard on yourself, Emmi. I said you have a beautiful body and I meant it. Maybe I'll have to show you how beautiful. But not until you shake off that bug you've picked up. How about some orange juice?"

"I could use a glass of water." He nodded and left the room. When he was gone, she lay back into her pillow and closed her eyes. *Damn, and double damn,* she said to herself. *Why do I have to have the stupid flu now of all times?* Were all the powers of heaven stacked against her having a love life? She was beginning to believe so.

When he came back with the water, she sipped it, then rested her head on the pillow. He brushed the hair back from her forehead and kissed it lightly.

"Get some sleep. It's about the only thing that helps. I'll see you later." When the bedroom door closed behind him, she cursed again. Finally she fell into a deep, feverish sleep. It was close to seven o'clock when her eyes opened again. She looked out the window. It was still raining and so cloudy the world was already in semidarkness. She sat up, put her bare feet on the floor, and took stock of herself. Better, she decided, much better and maybe just a bit hungry. Remembering some leftover soup in the fridge, she headed for the kitchen, not bothering with slippers or robe.

She was halfway there before she noticed him stretched out on her sofa, Bailly asleep beside him on the floor. How comfortable and at ease he looked, as though he belonged here, sleeping in her living room on a rainy Monday. How she envied him his quiet self-assurance. All her moves were accompanied by a jangling bunch of nerves. Except sometimes with Quinn.

She continued to study him. A book lay open across his broad chest, and one hand rested on Bailly's back. His hair was longer, she noticed. Uncut since coming to the island, she guessed. She badly wanted to touch it, feel it curl and wrap around her fingers as it did during those few moments last night. Hypnotized by his sleeping figure, she just stood there letting time and motion stop.

When Bailly decided to get up and come to her, the movement woke Quinn. His eyes opened on her, and he stared at her a long moment before giving her a slow, sexy smile. Emily saw a jagged bolt of blue lightning arc between them in the darkened room. It thudded against her chest with enough power to bend her ribs.

"Hi," he said, his eyes never leaving her face.

"Hi." She stared back as though in a trance.

"Feeling better?" He didn't move.

"I think so."

Emily blinked to break the spell. "I'm hungry—if that counts for anything."

She was also half naked she remembered suddenly.

Before she could turn to the bedroom to get her robe, Quinn was beside her.

"I'm a bit hungry, too. I'll fix us a sandwich. You take the sofa."

Emily didn't protest. She couldn't. Quinn's hands on her bare shoulders made her knees buckle. She'd been perfectly all right until then. She sank into the warmth left by his big body and the faint scent of his after-shave.

"There. Comfortable?" He tucked her under the light cotton coverlet she kept on the sofa for those reading nights by the fire.

"You're fussing over me. I'm fine now. Honestly."

"I like 'fussing' over you." When he moved to sit on the edge of the sofa, she shifted to make room. He leaned an arm on the back of the sofa and bent to look closely at her. He put his hand across her forehead. "Are you honestly feeling better? You feel a bit warm."

"I'm okay," she whispered, liking the feel of him against her, liking the light in his eyes when he looked at her.

Quinn caressed her face before dropping his hand to the hollow at the base of her throat. His eyes left hers to watch his index finger draw a line from her throat to the light coverlet that shielded her.

The coverlet offered no resistance, and his slow finger dragged it downward to uncover the rise of her lace-covered breasts. Looking at her creamy skin made his breath catch in his throat. Emily's skin was fantastic. His finger curled under the edge of the delicate lace, and he watched as her own rapid breathing caused her breasts to strain against the silk and lace, dark nipples hardening and poking at the snug bodice of her gown. God, how he wanted to touch them, more than touch, he thought as he wet his own dry lips, but it wasn't the right time. He pulled the light blanket back up to cover her, and his eyes again met hers. If he was going to do this, he was going to do it right. He hoped to God he wasn't making the worst mistake of his life, but he wanted this woman like no other, and he didn't intend to hurry. He drew in a deep lung-expanding breath and started to get up. Emily touched his arm.

"Why are you stopping?" Emily's gray eyes were direct.

He grinned. Trust Emily to be forthright. She was the oddest mixture of innocence and seduction he'd ever experienced. They were going to be wonderful together.

"You've been sick, remember. Besides, you and I are going to have a talk first."

"Does that mean you're going to . . . you know—"

"When you set your mind to something, you don't let go, do you?" He looked at her with a quizzical grin. "Should I be worried about my virtue here? Do you just want to have your way with me, then toss me aside?" He rested a hand on her shoulder and used his thumb to stroke her jawline.

Emily couldn't help the smile that claimed her face as she swept her eyes up to his. "Would that be so terrible?"

Suddenly the smile left Quinn's face "I'm not sure. I've never been used for exactly this purpose before."

Emily bolted upright and the thin coverlet dropped to her waist. She pulled it up and clutched it to her chest. "Oh, Quinn. I never thought about it that way. I didn't. It's because you're so special, so strong about things. It couldn't be just anyone. It has to be you. It's not about using—truly, it isn't."

"What's it about then?" Now that he thought about

it, the using part of this arrangement did bother him—
a little.

Emily paused before answering. "For me it's about
how I feel when you touch me. What I see in your
eyes. It's about a stumbling first step and who I want
to take that first step with. For you maybe it's as simple
as . . ." She watched him smile at her next words.
"Satisfaction for a job well done. You told me yourself, you're leaving in a month. A romantic encounter
with an island girl can't be too painful, can it? I mean
it's not *using* if everything is up front from the beginning, is it?"

"No, I suppose not. Besides, we're already having a
'romantic encounter,' or didn't you notice?" His thumb
whispered across the rise of her breast.

Emily drew in a long breath. "I noticed."

He pressed a kiss to the palm of her hand and smiled.
"But we still have to talk." He stood up. "And you
should eat. What's in that fridge of yours?"

"I'll help." She started to get up, then remembered
the revealing nightgown. When she wrapped the blanket
around her, she heard Quinn chuckle. What she saw
when she looked up was a pair of teasing blue eyes.

"Are you cold?" he asked.

"No, I'm, uh, . . ." She trailed off. She was always
trailing off, she thought, suddenly angry at herself. Seconds before she'd been calmly discussing how and
when she was going to make love with this man, and
now she was wrapping herself up like a mummy. He
must think her the most Victorian creature he'd ever
met. What an idiot she was.

"If you are feeling better and want to help, why
don't you go get dressed?" He reached for the edge of
the blanket and gave it a tug. "Clutching this thing in

the kitchen could be awkward. It might even fall off. You wouldn't want that, would you?"

Emily raised her eyes to his and took a silent breath. Without a word, she stood up, dropped the blanket, turned, and headed for her bedroom.

Quinn watched her walk away and wondered how much sexual frustration he could handle in the wait for the perfect time. He hadn't realized how lush she was. Was he imagining it, or was she thinner than when he'd first seen her a couple of weeks ago? Thin or no, she had the greatest . . . rear end he'd ever laid eyes on. She should be proud of that body and not be hiding it under baggy sweaters and blankets. Before this month was over, he vowed, she would be. He turned toward the kitchen and started to think about the next four weeks. The sale of his business was the last thing on his mind.

"Had enough?" Emily asked, rising to clear the plates. Quinn rose with her.

"Plenty, thanks. Does your fridge always show such a good yield. If it does, I might go foraging in there more often." He picked up his plate and followed her to the dishwasher.

"I like to cook. That's a bad habit when there's only one mouth to feed. Tends to make for a lot of leftovers. But I keep cooking anyway. Coffee?"

"I'll make it. That's about the only thing I'm expert at in the kitchen." He moved toward the coffeepot.

"Oh, I don't know. You did okay last night."

"If you like your potaotes rare and your steaks crisp, I guess you could say that." He grinned, pleased when he heard a trace of laughter with her smile.

"What about when you're at home? What do you cook there?"

"I don't. I eat out—a lot. I had a live-in cook, maid type for a while, but I was never home enough to keep her busy. I think she died from boredom, rambling around that big house with nothing to do."

"Where exactly do you live?" she asked.

"Malibu, mostly. But like I said, I'm away a lot. I also keep an apartment in New York, but I'm there even less than Malibu. But when I am, it's better than a hotel."

"How long have you been living like that?"

"Almost since the day I started Action Sports. Actually, the place at Malibu is my first stab at a permanent home, and I bought that only a couple years ago."

"Do you like it there?"

He turned from his task with the coffee to look at her. "I like the setting, the ocean, the sunsets, but the house doesn't feel much like a home."

"Why not?" Emily glanced up at him as she cleared the rest of the table.

"When I bought the place, I hired an interior decorator. I intended to work with her, seriously get into it, but I was too busy. Anyway, I finally just told her to go ahead and do what she thought best. The extent of my instructions was to do something homey." He looked around and swept a hand to take in Emily's house. "I meant like this—what I got was chintz and cabbage roses." He laughed at that. "It's not exactly *me* as they say in designer circles."

"Chintz and cabbage roses!" Emily's laughter blended with his. There was no way she could see this big powerful man surrounded by cabbage roses.

"I keep promising myself to fix it, but I haven't found the time."

"Your life sounds busy, very . . . full. Do you like it that way?"

"All in all? Yes, I do. I like action. Things happening around me. Though sometimes, lately, it's been too much even for me. Still, when Paul offered me his place here, I was damned nervous at the thought of all this peace and quiet."

"Salt Spring is a far cry from L.A., isn't it?" She remembered the pictures of Quinn in *Persona*, running in charity events, attending premieres. She leaned against the counter and wiped her hands with the tea towel, her gaze never leaving him.

"Yes, it is. And so far I've enjoyed every minute of it. There've been some pleasant surprises on this island. One in particular." He looked at her and grinned. "How come so many questions tonight, Emmi? You've asked me more in the last ten minutes than in the past two weeks." He moved toward her and took the tea towel from her hands. "Are you actually interested in me at last?"

Emily's expression turned sober. "I've been interested in you since the day I first saw you riding your bike in Ganges," she said without a thread of artifice.

"I like you, Emily Welland. Did you know that? I like you an awful lot." He kissed the tip of her nose, then hung up the towel. "The coffee will be a couple more minutes. Let's go sit down." His hands stroked down from her shoulders to grasp hers and lead her to the sofa.

SEVEN

When Emily tensed at even this friendly touch, she was again angry at herself. She wanted to be with Quinn more than anything else in the world, but she couldn't seem to stop these stabs of fear, the endless stream of anxieties that kept poking and pricking at her resolve. Gloriously happy one minute, then terrified, convinced she was frigid, that she could never please him. What if she couldn't arouse him? God, the man had been with Gina Manzoni for heaven's sake. She'd set herself up for making love with him. She would do it. What if he laughed at her? She couldn't bear it. If only she was experienced. *If you were experienced, you idiot, you wouldn't be throwing yourself at this man. God*, she thought then, *is that what I'm doing? Maybe I should* . . .

"I'd say a penny for those thoughts, but I get the feeling they're worth a lot more."

"I was thinking about—"

"Let me guess. You and me. Right?"

Emily nodded.

"And?" He urged her on, watching her face. It was tense and serious again. Quinn's stomach contracted. He'd never been with anyone as frightened and vulnerable as this woman. When she didn't answer, he went on.

"Nothing's going to happen, you know. Not tonight anyway. So you can relax. Maybe not tomorrow either or the day after that or the day after that."

Emily swung to look at him. "But you said you were going to—"

He stopped her by placing his index finger against her lips. "Emily, where did you get the idea everything is up to me? *I'm* not the only one involved here. You have something to do with it as well."

"Me?"

"I want a partner, not a passive receptor. Do you understand that? I want that for me, but I want it even more for you. I want you to reach for me, crave me the way I crave you. I want you to need me, and I want you to act on that need. Unafraid and . . . aggressive." Quinn wasn't sure that was the right word, but it would do.

"Aggressive? Me?" Her heart skidded to a stop. She was doomed.

When he saw the miserable expression on her face, Quinn took her face between his hands and gave her a smile of pure seduction. "Don't worry. I'll help the process along. But I want you easy with me, Emily, comfortable. At ease with your body and with mine. That takes time, especially for someone who has trouble even being seen in a nightgown with the man she wants to make love to," he teased. Emily blushed.

He stood up then and turned to look back at her. "There's one more thing. I want you to have a chance to change your mind. I'll stop any time you want me to, Emily. I want you to remember that. It may not be easy, but I'll stop. You have total control over what happens between us in the coming weeks. If you change your mind . . . *at any time* . . . tell me. Promise?" Quinn hoped he could keep his end of the bargain, to stop if she asked him to. He was honest; it sure as hell wouldn't be easy to call a halt to what was happening between them. Not for him at least.

She nodded.

"I want to hear you say it."

She looked up at him with a trace of stubborness. "I promise, but I'm not going to stop you." She wondered if any other woman went through this to go to bed with a man.

"I hope not. If you do, I'll be damned disappointed. Not to mention that my substantial male ego might be scarred forever."

"I have one question." She had to ask, had to. "Did you make Gina Manzoni run this gauntlet? Were there all these, uh, conditions?"

His smile died. "No."

"Why not?"

"Let's just say Gina isn't . . . you. I'll get the coffee." He turned abruptly and headed for the kitchen.

Emily sat on the sofa, picked up a cushion, punched it in irritation, then yanked it hard against her chest, wondering morosely why she couldn't be more like Gina. Aggressive. The word stuck in her brain like a broken arrow. She didn't want to wait for Quinn; she wanted him now. Maybe she could get him to . . . the thought sank as quickly as it surfaced, weighted down by anxieties and insecurities. She had no idea what to do. She heard Quinn come back with the coffee.

"By the way. Do you have someone who can take

over your store for a few days?" He handed her a steaming mug.

"Maybe. Why?"

"I thought we could do a bit of sightseeing, have some time together. I'd like to spend a couple of days in Victoria next time. I've never been there. Isn't there a famous hotel there . . . on the harbor?"

"The Empress."

"That's it. How about it? Want to show me your hometown?" He looked at her over the rim of his mug. "Who knows, maybe by then we can even share a room." His smile was back and there was no mistaking the tease in his tone.

Emily threw the pillow at him. He wanted aggressive, didn't he?

"Now that's new reading material for you, Em." Grace looked across the counter and tapped a finger on the book in front of Emily. "*Love and Sex,*" she read aloud, twisting her head to see better. "What's this, a crash course?"

"You might say that." Emily closed the book and gave Grace a good imitation of Mona Lisa. She didn't blush. Books never made her blush. "Grace, I've got a favor to ask. Can you look after the store for the next week? I'm going to have Marsha come in and cover for me, but she might need supervision. Would you mind?"

"No. I don't mind. What's up?" Grace's questioning look deepened. "Is it that gorgeous California man?"

"He wants me to show him more of the island and . . . maybe spend a couple of days in Victoria next week."

Grace took a long, hard look at her friend. She was glowing. There was a keen new light in her gray eyes that silvered and softened them at the same time. "You're sure about this, Em? Really, really sure? You've thought it through."

"I'm sure. And yes, I've thought it through a hundred, no, a thousand times. It's what I want. I'm happy, Grace. Happy in a way I've never been before." She beamed.

"All right then!" Grace gave her a solid thumbs-up sign. "That's great, Em. Absolutely great. Let's go shopping?"

"Shopping?" Emily echoed.

"Judging from the book you're reading and your plans for a few days off, I'm guessing you might be thinking of doing something more entertaining than run-of-the-mill sightseeing. Come on. If we hurry, we can make the next ferry to Victoria. I know where there's this great lingerie shop and—"

"You're kidding. We can't leave . . . just like that. What about the stores?"

"Damn the stores. This is Salt Spring Island, remember. They've seen 'gone fishin' ' signs before."

When Emily started to protest again, Grace raised her hand. "Not another word. I'm going to freeze muffin dough. You, my dear, are going to close your till. We're going shopping for the sexiest underwear we can find. You don't want to be caught wearing industrial underpants. Do you?"

Emily blushed.

At seven o'clock, Emily was struggling through shopping bags to open her front door. The Victoria spree went beyond underwear to blouses, skirts, new slacks—a whole size smaller than normal, she noted gleefully—shoes, and another nightgown. Emily shook her head as she dumped the purchases on her bed. *I may have to sell the store to pay for this,* she thought, the unlikely prospect not fazing her at all. She hadn't had so much fun in ages.

It was the first time she'd ever gone shopping with a man in mind, an incredibly sexy man with navy blue eyes and dark wavy hair. It was amazing how thinking about Quinn influenced her choices. She would never have bought the ridiculously expensive lace blouse with the high neck and row of tiny pearl buttons down the back without him in mind. Nor would she have considered the calf-length midnight blue velvet skirt that went so well with it. Emily loved the antique look of the outfit and couldn't wait to wear it for him. Maybe for dinner at the Empress, she mused. Looking at the new clothes made her feel more confident, more womanly. She was starting to fold them when the phone rang. It was Quinn.

"You're back from your fishing trip, I see." His voice was deep and intimate even through phone wire.

Her heart speed picked up and she marveled again at the physical reactions he never failed to evoke. "Fishing? Oh. Those signs were Grace's idea. We, uh, went shopping." Emily was holding a strip of satin in her hand that had miraculously been turned into a bra.

"Shopping, huh? I hope you bought something X rated." Quinn laughed. He could see her turn red through the phone. Her answer as usual surprised him.

"As a matter of fact, I did. Enough silk and satin for my next half-dozen affairs."

It was his turn to feel anxious. "You planning on making this a habit, Emily?"

"For the time being . . . maybe." She twirled the satin bra in the air, feeling wanton at the thought of wearing it. "What did you do today?" she asked.

"You mean besides haunting the Welland bookstore?

Not much. Spent most of the day thinking about you.''
He paused. "Have you eaten?''

"Not yet. Would you like to come for dinner?''
Emily tried to imagine what would come to mind when
Quinn thought about her. The idea of occupying space
inside his head was appealing—very appealing.

"I thought we'd go out. Hastings House. How does
that sound?''

"I'd love it! I hate to admit it, but in all the time
I've lived on the island, I've never been there.'' *Mainly
because I can't afford it,* she thought. Hastings House
with its rustically beautiful waterfront accommodation
and gourmet dining room was both elegant and expensive. And, from what Emily heard, worth every penny.

"Good, we can discover it together then. I'll pick
you up in an hour. Is that enough time?''

"An hour will be fine.''

After she'd hung up the phone, Emily looked at the
clothes strewn over her bed with renewed interest. Her
decision was fast. The black cotton jersey, simple and
comfortable. She headed for the shower.

She was five minutes from ready when she heard a
knock on the front door. Opening her bedroom door
long enough to yell "Come in,'' she ducked back
to her mirror and finished her makeup. She couldn't
remember when she'd last taken an hour to get ready—
for anything. Ten minutes was her personal best. She
smoothed the clinging black fabric over her hips and
adjusted the scooped neckline. A slash of lipstick and
she was done.

"You look beautiful, Emmi.'' Quinn's eyes were
dark with admiration as he took in the simple dress
with the touch of cotton lace at the neckline. He decided Emily and lace were made for each other.

"Thank you. So are you.''

He laughed, but she meant it. He *was* beautiful. Dressed in navy slacks, a white shirt, and a deep-blue sweater, and with his dark hair grazing the sharp edge of his collar, he was so beautiful he made her ache. She wanted to walk over and kiss him, ever so lightly on those softly smiling lips. *Do it, Emmi,* she told herself, but she didn't. She stared at him instead.

"Now that we've decided we're both 'beautiful people' shall we go?" he asked.

"I'll get my coat."

When he'd helped her on with it, he pulled her back to his chest and kissed her lightly on the neck.

"Hm, mm, you smell good. Too good." He nuzzled her throat and took another breath before stepping back and turning her to face him. He was smiling when he spoke, but his eyes were grave. "I think this 'romantic encounter' with an island girl could end up being more than I bargained for. I also think it's a good thing we're going to be in public tonight."

At that moment, Emily would have been more than content to stay right where they were. Her knees were weak from being close to him. She was tempted to say that, but Quinn was opening the door. In seconds they were in the Range Rover headed to Ganges. She smiled inwardly. *He does have to bring me home after dinner,* she mused.

The evening was . . . Emily searched for the right word and decided on glorious. She glanced at Quinn's shadowy profile in the night-darkened car. He drove in a silence as complete as her own, his right hand resting idly on the wheel as the left steered from below. Closing her eyes, she let her head fall against the backrest.

Glorious, she said again and started to play the evening back, scene by scene, setting the memories firmly in place. There was the light squeeze Quinn gave her shoulder when he helped her off with her coat. His hand on the small of her back as they walked to the table. The way he'd tilted his head and smiled at her as he studied the wine list. Candlelight shadows on his upturned palm when he'd reached across the table to silently ask for her hand. A hand she gave willingly. Then his eyes, hot and dark, gazing at her across his warmed brandy glass. Without warning, a sense of loss crept over her, followed by a painful sadness. Her timidity, her damned phobias caused her to miss so much these past years. .

There could have been other nights like this one had she not been shackled by her own weaknesses. She looked again at the man beside her, his strong profile outlined by the moonlight at the car window, and the regret vanished. One thing was sure, there could never have been another Quinn. Maybe it was meant to be, she mused. Maybe it was the hand of fate that brought him to her island now, for this brief time.

How could she stand to see him leave? She cut off the thought, refusing to think about it. Tonight, now, this moment, and the moments of the next few weeks would have to be enough. She would not, could not lay further claim to him. No commitments, no strings, she owed him that. His warm hand grasped hers.

"You're too quiet." He took his eyes from the road long enough to appraise her melancholy look. "Why so serious? You did enjoy dinner, didn't you?"

"Oh, yes. I loved it. It was a beautiful evening."

"I'm glad. I wanted you to enjoy it. But your words don't match the expression on your face. A good description would be pensive, I think. Second thoughts— about us?" Quinn was afraid of her answer. He was determined to give her time to think, to back out if she wanted to. It was, after all, a most unconventional agreement they'd made. Suddenly he was afraid she would back out, change her mind. His stomach clenched when he looked at her innocent face. He knew he was rapidly developing a paranoia about hurting her. *Be honest,* he said to himself, *she's becoming more important to you with every moment you spend together.* Again he told himself to take it slow, excruciatingly slow. In a few weeks, he'd be leaving.

She took a long time to answer. She was having second thoughts, but they weren't ones Quinn needed to worry about. Emily's thoughts only confirmed her desire for him, her love for him. She would have him, love him, and watch him go back to the life he came from. She would do it if it killed her.

"Second thoughts? A few. But none of them are fearful, and none of them have an ounce of regret. You?" Emily tried to sound casual and ignore her twittering stomach.

Quinn pulled into her driveway and stopped the car. He turned to her. "I don't want to hurt you. It would kill me to hurt you. You know I have to go back to L.A. Everything I have, everything I am, is there." His voice was studiously determined, and his eyes searched her for response.

"I know," she said simply. "I told you, Quinn, I understand. Don't be afraid. I promise you I won't break, I won't fall apart. I only need . . ." She wanted to say, "You. I need you, Quinn," but stopped herself. "I need something from you. That doesn't mean I'm going to lay claim to your life." She lifted her head. "Nor do I want you to lay claim to mine. An act of physical love doesn't have to be a chain around either of our necks. All I want is something . . . beautiful." She was pleased at how modern she sounded, hoping she'd hit the right note. This was getting too serious. She smiled up at his serious face and tried for levity. "Besides, if you expect me to be aggressive, it may never happen."

When he saw her smile, he took her in his arms and gathered her close. His breath warmed her and his low voice stilled her as he gazed down at her half-open lips. "It's going to happen, all right. Nothing in the world could stop it. And it will be beautiful, Emmi. I promise you that. You're a desirable, intriguing woman, and it would take a better man than I am to deny you—anything." He kissed her lightly and smiled against her lips. "Least of all my body that reacts at the slightest touch, slightest look from you." He took her hand and held it palm flat against his heart. "Feel that? Feel what you do to me?" he whispered against her throat.

Emily's breath came in uncontrollable gusts from her lungs. When he placed her hand on his chest, her own heart stopped completely. The heat of him, the harsh pounding of his heart intoxicated her. The mat of his chest hair was springy under the soft cotton of his shirt. Gently she scraped her long nails across it. She closed her eyes, heightening her sense of him, absorbing him. When she felt the tightening between her legs, she sighed and, in an unthinking rush of movement, wrapped her arms around his neck and nestled her head under his chin. With her ear close to his heart, the pounding grew louder. Her fingers caressed the soft hair at his nape, then moved upward, reveling in its thickness.

"Quinn, oh, Quinn . . . I love the feel of you." She lifted her eyes to his. "I love the—"

His mouth took hers. His movement restless, demanding. He flicked his tongue along the line of her lips, then probed inward, seeking, playing, dancing.

Emily's heart pounded, and a moist heat built between her thighs. Moaning, she squirmed and pressed close, her tongue loving his, meeting it stroke on stroke. The soft sound of her pleasure made him groan. Roughly, he crushed her to him before shuddering his frustration into her shoulder.

"I think we should stop," he said in a hoarse voice. "When we make love, it isn't going to be in the front seat of a Range Rover." One more second of this and Quinn knew he would lose control. He was quickly coming to understand he didn't have much when it came to this gray-eyed woman. But like it or not, this wasn't the time. He swore inwardly.

Emily sighed and pulled away, her fingers reluctant to leave his soft, thick hair, her mouth damp from his kisses. God, he felt so good. She wanted to touch him all over. He was driving her crazy.

"I don't want to stop, and we don't have to stay in this car. I have a . . ." she gulped, "a perfectly good, uh, bed not a dozen steps away." She blushed furiously, but she'd said it and she was glad.

"I know you do, and I want to be in it—with you. But I'm leaving tomorrow, very early, and I don't want to have to run away from you."

"Leaving? I don't understand." She was stunned. He'd said nothing about leaving during dinner.

"Only for a few days. Three if I can get everything done that I have to."

"But why?"

"It seems the potential buyers for my business have come up with a few more questions. Questions I can't handle by phone, but I should be back by Friday at the latest if all goes well. I'll call you. Okay?" He searched her face for irritation or disappointment but saw none. He stifled a faint sense of hurt.

Ignoring the sharp pain in her chest, Emily recalled her earlier vow. She would make no claims on his life. Better learn to start right now, she told herself. This is a dry run of what you'll have to face later. She smiled into his eyes and surprised herself by reaching out her hand and brushing his hair gently over his ear.

"You don't have to call. Just come back when you're ready. Neither the island nor I is going anywhere."

Quinn stared out the plane window into the pale yellow air of L.A. He was oddly disoriented. If this was home, why did he feel as though he'd left the best behind? An ironic smile curled his lips. He'd left here two weeks ago filled with questions, and here he was two weeks later coming back with even more. And none of them concerned his business. They had to do with a certain island girl, bookstore owner, playwright—and what? What exactly was she to him? And how had she managed to get under his skin? They had nothing in common. Their lives were completely different. He couldn't see Emily leaving her precious island to live in L.A. She'd be miserable here. He stopped. Where the hell did that thought come from?

He leaned back into the seat. *You're starting to fantasize*, he told himself. *She hasn't been out of your mind since you left the island*. He missed her—so damned much—he couldn't believe it. *What was needed here was a diversion*, he decided. *Something or, better still, someone to take your mind off her*. The smart thing to do was spend the next couple of days looking for just that. This was California. If he couldn't find a diversion here, he wouldn't find it anywhere.

"Would you please put your seat in the upright position, sir," the flight attendant said. "We'll be landing shortly."

Quinn nodded and secured his seat belt. A diversion. Yes. There were lots of those in L.A.

That evening Emily sat on her log with a steaming mug of coffee in her hand and thought about Quinn Ramsay. She'd thought of nothing else all day. She sighed. The next few days would be the longest of her life. Her eyes strayed to Bailly. Pawing in the sand, he began anew his endless search for the tiny crabs that scuttled about under the beach rocks. She'd never yet seen him catch one and wasn't at all sure he wanted to. She watched him tilt his head as he uncovered yet another of the odd creatures for his curious examination. He was fascinated. *I know all about fascination, Bailly, old boy,* she thought, when a pair of blue eyes came to mind.

Emily chided herself for not being at her computer. Granger was getting impatient. He wanted a couple of minor changes in the second act, and he said he needed them for tomorrow night. With only two weeks before opening night, he had every right to be impatient. But she didn't want to work tonight. She wanted to dream. Dream about Quinn coming back, the time they would have together. Dream about his arms around her, the man scent of him, his mouth, his eyes, the way he looked at her. He colored her world, dominated it, and for now, this special time, she was content with that.

She gazed at the flat face of the sky and watched the sun's lazy descent, wondering if Quinn was watching this same scene from his Malibu deck. The idea cheered her. She stood up then, brushed the back of her jeans, and headed in. Duty prodded and guilt pushed. Granger needed his words.

* * *

Quinn stood in the living room of the luxurious Beverly Hills home and took a long pull on his drink. It wasn't yet midnight, but he'd had all of this party he could take. It was time to go home.

He heard a bright laugh and glanced again at the attractive brunette in the lime-green dress. One narrow strap fell and looped over a softly rounded shoulder. She appeared to be listening to the conversation of her male companion, but she was looking at Quinn. The laugh was for him, as was the invitation in her artfully made-up eyes. Eyes that hadn't left him since his arrival an hour ago. At first she piqued his interest. He was here for a diversion, wasn't he? There was no doubt in his mind this woman would be a blue-ribbon distraction.

He was still thinking about it when Paul stepped to his side and asked, "Want to tell me who she is?"

Quinn shrugged and glanced again at the laughing woman. "I don't know. It's your party. Don't you know your own guests?"

Paul inclined his head toward the brunette. "I don't mean her."

Quinn took another drink and gave his friend a questioning look. "Who then?"

"The woman on your mind. Anybody I know?"

"What makes you think I've got a woman on my mind?"

"I know the look. It can take me days to get that look in front of a camera. Kind of an interesting cross between frustration and confusion. Been there often enough myself."

"Hate to disappoint you, but I was thinking about my meeting tomorrow. As a matter of fact, I think I'll clear out of here, get some sleep."

"Alone?" Paul nodded toward the brunette. "I'd say the way she's ogling you, that shouldn't be necessary."

"Alone," Quinn growled as he finished his drink.

Paul smiled the kind of knowing smile only a good friend can give another. "I'm impressed already. She must be one fascinating woman to make *you* go willingly to a lonely bed."

"Say good night, Paul," Quinn demanded tersely.

Paul laughed at the scowl on his friend's face. "Good night, pal. Sleep . . . loose."

EIGHT

"I didn't know you played hooky, Emmi. I wouldn't have thought you were the type. Far too responsible."

Emily spun around, then leaped to her feet. "Quinn! You're back." She was standing now only a couple of feet from him but felt strangely timid again. He was so perfect standing there in freshly washed jeans and a snowy white shirt. She was filthy, having spent the morning grubbing in the garden, then filling her window boxes with geraniums and petunias.

He gave her a megawatt smile. "Yes, I'm back. A day late but back." *Thank God*, he said to himself as he looked at her. She looked incredible. Torn jeans, dirty hands, hair tied back with a piece of leather, bare feet, face smudged with garden soil. The four days had felt like months. He'd hoped she would throw her arms around him. Instead she was shy again and hesitant. Then he looked at her; there was no hesitancy in her eyes.

"Come here," he said gruffly, reaching out a hand. She moved toward him and stopped. "I'm all dirty."

"I don't care if you're covered in tar. Come here. I want to hold you. I missed you—really missed you."

Emily gave him a look of pure sunshine and ran to his arms. "Oh, Quinn. I missed you, too. You can't imagine how much."

He hugged her to him long and hard, and for a time, neither of them spoke.

Emily realized she was still clutching her hand spade, and she was making an awful mess of his shirt. She pulled away. "Look what I've done." She tried to rub off the dirt. "Oh, damn, I'm making it worse." She stepped back.

He laughed. "I've got other shirts. Don't worry about it." He grasped both her hands and lifted them around his neck. "Can't you think of anything better to do with those hands? Something, uh, . . . more aggressive."

She looked up into his eyes, and it was her turn to laugh. "Maybe I can at that," she said as she pulled his mouth to hers.

He sighed into her parted lips and pulled her hard against his body. "That's more like it," he whispered when the kiss finished and he was nuzzling her throat. "Much more like it."

"Now I've made your face dirty." She was looking at him with shining eyes. "Anyone would think you'd spent the afternoon mud wrestling." Again she rubbed at the dirt, and again she made it worse. "I give up," she said then. "You'll have to come in and wash up. When did you get back? Have you eaten? I've baked fresh bread. I can make you a sandwich."

"Sounds good, but for now come with me. I brought you something." He grabbed her mucky hand and pulled her up the driveway. "I'm parked up on the road. I wanted to surprise you."

When they got to his Range Rover, he opened the back and brought out a bike. A silver-gray woman's mountain bike. It was beautiful and exactly the right size.

She grasped the handlebars and looked up at him. He had the expression of a young boy, pleased and expectant. She grinned in delight. "I love it, Quinn. I love it because it's from you and because . . . it has no crossbar."

He threw back his head and laughed. When he looked back at her, she was already on the bike heading down her driveway, waving him to follow.

She was propping the bike up against the house by the time he reached her.

"Now tell me. When did you get back?"

"About an hour ago. And in answer to your next question, I haven't eaten and I'm starved."

"You don't look starved." *I'm the one who's starved*, she thought, *starved for you*. "But why don't you check out the fridge, see what you'd like. I'll have a quick shower and we'll eat outside. It's too good a day to waste indoors."

"Sounds good." Again he pulled her close; she went willingly. "But don't be too long, okay? I'm even more starved for you than I am for a sandwich."

Emily looked at him in surprise. He had mirrored her thoughts exactly. She scooted to her bathroom, determined to make this the shortest shower on record.

By the time she made it back to the kitchen, Quinn was coming from outside. He already had the sandwich fixings on the patio. He stopped when he saw her, inhaled sharply, and ran a hand down the length of her wet, slick hair. "You look great. Good enough to—" he stopped, his eyes darkening as he gazed down at her. "Good enough for anything." He paused again and ran his knuckles lightly along her jawline. "Tomorrow," he said suddenly. "Tomorrow we go to Victoria. Okay?"

There was no mistaking his intent.

"Tomorrow," she answered, trying to keep her voice and eyes steady as a shudder of raw sexual excitement shook her to her toes.

He continued to gaze on her as if in a trance, his expression rapt and hungry. Emily felt a curious chill, followed by a rush of warmth. Her eyes stayed on his until he took another deep breath.

"Tomorrow." His smile melted her. "First I want to talk. I want to hear what you've been up to since I've been gone. How's the play going? It opens next Saturday, right?"

". . . Right. Saturday. There's a dress rehearsal this Wednesday." Emily took two mugs down from the cupboard and attempted to cross the emotional bridge from passionate fantasy to reality. It wasn't easy when the word "tomorrow" echoed through her head with the resonance of a high Alps yodel. She could scarcely hear the sound of her own voice.

"Will we be going?"

"Going?" she repeated absently.

"To the dress rehearsal. I'd like to go with you. Or don't they allow outsiders?" He was reaching into the fridge. "Aha! Strawberries." He headed to the door and Emily followed, carrying the mugs.

She hadn't thought about his seeing her play. Not at the dress rehearsal or any other time. It hadn't occurred to her he would be interested. When they were at the door, she asked, "You'd really like to come?" Her words were softly spoken and laced with amazement.

"Yes, is that a problem? I want to go to the opening

too. Assuming, of course, there's no black tie required. I left that in L.A.'' He grimaced broadly.

Emily laughed. "No to both questions. It's not a problem and it's definitely not black tie. More like blue jeans and sneakers.''

"Perfect.'' He reached for the mustard.

Emily watched him put together a sandwich and smiled.

He caught her looking at him and grinned back. "Aren't you going to eat?''

"No. I'm not hungry. You go ahead.'' She continued to study him, drink him in. She was also trying to figure out what was different about him. She decided to ask.

"You're very . . . happy today,'' she said. "Did your meetings go well?'' She leaned back in the old Cape Cod chair and watched his face.

"Very well. It seems my decision to take this Salt Spring *sabbatical* has worked in my favor. The buyer has upped the offer. I guess they thought I was going to turn them down, that coming here was a delaying tactic or some kind of negotiating ploy.''

"Was it?''

"No. I honestly needed to think. The first offer was enough. I didn't need any added incentive.'' He grinned at her. "Not that I'm going to turn them down, you understand.''

She looked across the rim of her coffee cup. "You've decided then?''

"Almost. I guess my decision is ninety-nine percent made. I have a couple of things to check out and that will be that.''

"You know what you're going to do then . . . after the sale?''

He gave her a look she couldn't read. "I know what

I'd *like* to do, but I'm not sure yet whether it will work out. Like I said, I have a few things to check out. But so far things look good.'' He smiled then. ''From where I sit they look damned good.''

''I'm happy for you. It all sounds exciting and . . . mysterious, like you're about to embark on a grand adventure.'' She didn't ask any more questions. Quinn's business was *his* business. It had nothing to do with her. His next comment only added to her curiosity.

''A grand adventure?'' He seemed to ponder the words. ''God, Emmi, I'd like to think so. Adventure—and challenge—is exactly what I need.'' He stood up, taking a quick glance at his watch. He was a man in a hurry. ''Now let's clean up here. We've got time for a quick trial run with that new bike before I have to go.''

Emily wasn't actress enough to hide her disappointment. ''You're leaving . . . again?''

''I have to catch a plane in three hours. I'll only be gone overnight. I have a dinner meeting tonight and breakfast meeting early tomorrow. I'm sorry, Em, but I have to go. The guy I'm meeting is on a tight schedule. I probably should have stayed in Vancouver today, but I wanted to see you. I figured a couple of hours was better than nothing. Besides, I was hungry and I couldn't resist the thought of your fridge.'' He was trying to prod her out of her momentary depression. ''Is that look on your face telling me you can't live without me for another night?''

''I can, but I'm not sure I want to,'' she answered honestly. *We have so few nights, so very few*, she thought with an aching sadness.

''Tomorrow, Emily. Okay?'' He stroked her face.

Emily still couldn't settle down. It had been two hours since Quinn left, and before long it would be dark. Restless and moody, she decided to go for another bike ride. She was amazed at what a difference it made to have a bike the right size. She was actually enjoying it, and Bailly loved running alongside her.

"If we keep this up, Bailly, we'll both be in great shape."

They'd turned left on Morningside when she saw James. She smiled and waved, and Bailly went to say hello.

"Hi, Emmi. Quinn gone?" James got right to the point as always.

"Uh-huh. He'll be back tomorrow like he told you. He says you're doing real well, James."

Quinn had spent an hour with James before leaving for Vancouver, and he was planning to spend more time with him before they left for Victoria. It pleased her that he was so dedicated to coaching him. She was glad it hadn't been a passing whim, though she knew James was becoming attached to Quinn, maybe too attached, and would be as disappointed as her when he left. Lynn said not to worry about it, that he had to learn to say good-bye like the rest of us.

The boy beamed. "He gave me these." James lifted his left foot and pointed it toward her. It wasn't the first time he'd told her about his running shoes. She pretended it was.

"They're real nice. I bet you can beat anybody wearing those shoes."

"Quinn says I'm gonna win. If I try real hard, I'll win. Want me to show you what he taught me?"

"Sure." Emily leaned on her bike and watched James take his start position, then hurtle down the road. He was fast, she thought, and he was motivated. Thanks to Quinn.

"That's great, James. Really great."

"Guess what? I'm gonna run in another race after this one. In . . ." he stopped to think for a minute. "August. It's in Vancouver. August in Vancouver," he repeated before going on. "Quinn says he'll help me. He says the games are important—really important. They have gold and silver medals and everything. Not just ribbons."

"I don't think—" Emily stopped. James must have his dates confused. Quinn would be gone by August, long gone. Still it wasn't like James to have it wrong. When he was told a date or month, he always remembered it. He might not be able to relate it to the length of time, but he remembered the specifics. Had Quinn misled him in an effort to be kind? She didn't believe that. She wouldn't like to see James disappointed. Probably just a mistake, she concluded.

"Ja-ames. Ja-ames." It was Lynn calling. Emily looked at her watch. Nearly seven-thirty.

"You'd better go, hon. Your mom's calling."

"Okay. You coming to see me race next Saturday?"

"I hope so. But only the hundred meter. I can't stay for the relay. I have to get back to help with my play."

"You come with Quinn, okay?" he instructed.

"Okay. Now you'd better get going before your mom gets mad at you for being late."

James ran back down the road, spun around once to wave, and ran on. Lynn had told her how thrilled he was about the weekend games, but Emily hadn't realized how excited he was until now. He was completely focused on them. She hoped he would win. Maybe Quinn Ramsay was going to make both her and James winners. The thought cheered her, and she threw her right leg easily over the seat of her bike and cycled away.

*　　*　　*

The seaplane pitched and tossed as it came in for a landing on the choppy waters at the Vancouver terminal. Quinn looked at his watch. He had less than half an hour to get to his room at the Four Seasons, change, and make his dinner meeting. He would probably be a few minutes late. No matter. Claude would wait. He hailed a cab. When it pulled to the curb, he opened the door and tossed in his overnighter.

"Four Seasons," he told the driver, then settled into the seat.

He smiled to himself, anticipating the surprise on Claude's face when he hit him up for money. It would be a first, that was for sure, as this meeting was. Claude Christopher and Quinn Ramsay hadn't sat down together for at least ten years. They'd been too busy trying to beat each other up in the marketplace.

Quinn could imagine his longtime competitor's curiosity. He had told him very little when he'd called him in L.A., only that he had a proposition that would be good for both of them. Naturally, Claude would assume he was talking money *in*, not money going out.

Quinn leaned back in the seat. He felt edgy, but it was a good edgy. For the first time in years, he was excited about something. Something meaningful. He hoped Claude would feel the same. His support wasn't critical to the project, but it would speed the start-up phase. Quinn was impatient to tell Emily his plans, but that would wait until everything was set. He still had *i*'s to dot and *t*'s to cross.

It was too bad he hadn't been able to meet with Claude in Los Angeles, but his schedule had made it impossible. Quinn knew all about that kind of schedule and was grateful when his crusty competitor agreed to a stopover in Vancouver. Otherwise it would have been back to L.A. and away from Emily—again.

He didn't want to be away from Emily. That decision was made during a couple of long, restless nights in Malibu. He didn't want to be away from her—period. But he wasn't sure about her feelings. No matter how close they came, he sensed a distance in her, a protective reserve. In the next few days, he was determined to find out what that meant. She cared for him; he knew that. The question was—how much?

Tomorrow. Tomorrow he would find out. He had kept his word, given Emily ample time to think things through. The whole damned process had wreaked hell on his libido, but he hadn't rushed her. He'd done a hell of a lot of deep breathing, taken a cold shower or two, but he hadn't rushed her. He'd scarcely touched her, for God's sake! Today, when she'd pulled his mouth to hers for the first time, he'd almost lost it. It was the first overtly sexual move she'd made toward him. He could still feel her pressed against his length. She had to have felt how aroused he was. He shook his head and stared out the cab window.

He wanted their first time to be unique, out of the ordinary, and very, very special, not a quick coupling with no words, no time, and no promises. Emily deserved more, and he was going to make certain she got it.

"Miss me?" Quinn asked wrapping his arms round her from behind. He'd come back to the house after coaching James. Emily was in her bedroom packing.

She turned in his arms and smiled. "You've only been gone an hour," she teased. "But I'll admit to a touch of jealousy. What is it between you and James anyway?"

"The bonding of two jocks. What can I say?"

"If I take up a sport, would you coach me, bond with me, the way you do with James?"

"That's exactly what I'm going to do. Coach you— in the most beautiful hotel room Victoria has to offer. As for the bonding, that takes two, remember." He kissed her nose, not trusting himself with any other part of her anatomy. "But before anything, I need a shower. Do you mind? If I hurry, we should be able to catch the next ferry."

Emily nodded in the direction of the bathroom. When he went in and closed the door, she sat heavily on the edge of her bed. She rubbed her arms where his hands had been and sighed. She didn't want to wait another minute for Quinn Ramsay. Tonight was too far away. There must be something she could do. Their time was so precious, so short. Her heart started to pound, an alternating rhythm of fear and excitement. Could she do it? Dare she do it? Aggressive, that's what he kept saying. She stood up and started to take off her clothes. Aggressive was what he'd get. She dropped her T-shirt on the floor and closed her eyes. *Good-bye, shy Emily*, she said to herself.

Quinn felt her before he saw her. His shock was quickly replaced by excitement when he felt her shower-slicked arms wrap around him and her trembling body against his back. He knew she had crossed a boundary to come into the shower. Her pounding heart was testament to that. He turned and smiled down at her, making no secret of his own pleasure.

"This is much better than showering alone." He pulled her close and ran a caressing hand down her back. The heat came strong and fast, and Quinn leaned against the shower wall, pulling her with him. *Slow, Quinn, take it slow*, he said to himself. Right now, at this moment, he could have moved with a speed that would have scared the daylights out of her. He had to take it easy.

"You feel good, lady, damn good." His voice was rough velvet as he kissed her wet hair and smooth throat.

At his words, the touch of his hand, she relaxed. She knew then that she'd been terrified he would reject her. Instead he welcomed her, and she nestled against him, relishing the feel of skin against skin as the shower pulsed against her back. Quinn's skin was sleek with water and soap, and she ran her hands up the tight cords of his forearms. So firm. So strong. He was magnificent.

At her tentative touch, Quinn leaned his head back against the shower wall and closed his eyes. He knew she was exploring him, and he didn't want her to stop. He didn't want her ever to stop.

Her hands moved to his chest, and she pulled back to look at it, spreading her fingers to run her hands flat palmed through the damp hair on his chest. Curly hair that veed to the level plane of his stomach. Her palms started to follow the vee downward. When Quinn tensed, they stopped, veered off to run down the sides of his thighs. Emily raised dazzled, dreamy eyes to his as she brought her hands back to the expanse of his chest, lightly skimming his nipples. His hands, until now resting under iron restraint at the curve of her waist, suddenly dug into her soft flesh.

"Emmi," he started but couldn't finish when her pink tongue flicked out, first at one flat nipple, then the other. A lick. A taste. A nibble as she took one between her teeth. He was letting her play with him, and she was taking full advantage of it.

"Emmi," he said again, his voice darker and richer than she remembered. "Do you know what you're doing?"

She lifted her head from his chest and smiled. "Not exactly. What am I doing?" Her answer was a study in applied innocence.

Quinn managed a twisted smile. "You're raising my temperature at a rate of fifty degrees a second, and I think you damn well know it."

His hands moved down to her buttocks, and he pulled her to him—hard, his powerful arousal firm and strong against her. He'd half expected her to draw back. Instead she arched into him and ran a hand down between them to the crease at the top of his thigh, frighteningly close to the source of Quinn's control problem.

"That's it," he gasped. "Let's get out of this shower." When he reached over to turn off the tap, Emily's eyes caught him.

She reached up and took his face in her hands. "I don't want to wait, Quinn. I want to make love— now."

Emily could read the desire in his eyes, hear it in the raw huskiness of his voice when he answered. "I think I've got the idea, Emmi, but we're going to disappoint a lot of people.

Her face was questioning.

Quinn smiled at her, took a large white towel from the rack, and started to dry her. Taking his time, he rubbed down her back to her wet buttocks. "First, there's the hotel reservation. We said we'd be there by seven." He was drying the back of her thighs, moving the towel downward. When he reached her calves, he started up again, taking the inside route.

"We can sleep on a park bench," Emily murmured, struggling for breath. The struggle was lost when Quinn slipped the soft towel through her legs, bringing it to the sensitive juncture of her thighs. With aching slowness he dried her there before turning her to face him.

At the rapt expression on her face, his smile deepened. He decided she wasn't quite dry enough.

"Then there's dinner," he went on. "You know how maître d's can be when you show up late."

Emily's eyes were closed, and as with her teasing lover, food was the last thing on her mind. She would have told him that if he would quit playing with the towel.

His teasing stopped when he looked at her breasts, full and high, still shining with shower water. He couldn't bring himself to cover them with the towel. Instead, he openly admired them, dropping the towel to gently stroke and then cup them, testing weight and contour. They were, as he knew they would be, perfection in his hands.

Not content to hold, he explored, moving his hands until a bud from each breast touched the center of each palm. Gently, softly, barely keeping contact with her nipples, he rotated his hands. The sensation in her breasts was electric, and Emily closed her eyes against the hot surge of her arousal and let her head fall back. She gasped as her knees sagged and a sharp, warm sweetness filled the space between her legs. When she could stand it no more, she fell into Quinn's arms.

"Let's get to the damn bed," he growled. He stopped long enough to get a flat silver package from his shaving kit before picking her up and carrying her out of the steamy bathroom. He remembered his noble words to her, spoken only days ago. Words about stopping any time she said so. He wouldn't like to be put to the test. Not now with the blood raging through his veins with such unholy force his muscles ached. Not now, when he was so hot his flesh was melting. He wanted to be in her, so far, so deep that he'd touch her center.

When he reached the bed, he laid her down, dark eyes scanning, setting in memory the curves of her body. Emily's body. Again he admired her breasts before his eyes rested on the patch of dark hair between her legs. With an intensity new to him, he blazed with need, stark and raw. The force of it glinted from his eyes.

"Quinn?" When she saw the way he was looking at her, Emily reddened. She closed her legs and shifted to her side, using an arm to cover her breasts.

Quinn sat on the edge of the bed. "Don't, honey, I want to look at you. All of you."

He lifted her arm and with gentle pressure moved her to her back again. His eyes swept over her, bold, hungry, and blatantly sensuous. Pinning both arms above her head, he bent his own head to brush soft kisses on her throat and breasts before again lifting his eyes to hers.

"You're beautiful, sweetheart. Every curving, sexy inch of you." He touched her breast, rubbing the nipple with a firm, rhythmic movement. His thumb was gentle, but still her nipple jumped and hardened. She sighed, moaned, and gave small cries at his every touch. She surged into his caress, and her excitement, her innocent abandon, almost undid him. His groin tensed when he thought it could tense no more.

"I want to touch you. Touch all of you. Are you going to let me, Emmi?" He ran his hand down and across her stomach, then back to roll the other nipple between his thumb and forefinger. She was on fire. Still his eyes held hers looking for an answer.

She stroked her tongue over her dry lips, then placed her hand over his at her breast, stopping its seduction. She took a deep breath. "If you want me to talk, you can't do that."

"What about this?" He lowered his head, licked the hardened bud of her nipple, then took it fully into his mouth. She cried with pleasure as he sucked, pulling her nipple deep into his mouth and stroking it with the soft sandpaper of his tongue. She was at that moment—gone.

When he heard her moan, heard the soft growl of her sexual yearning, he lifted his head from the moist, swollen tip and shifted from the edge of the bed to lie beside her. Spiraling kisses up from her breasts to her throat, he took her mouth. His tongue thrust, penetrating as the rigid length of him throbbing hard against her thigh ached to do.

Emily, aroused to a fever unknown to her, was coming apart, drifting on a sea of physical sensations so new, so alarming that her only haven was Quinn's body. She dragged her nails across his back and cried his name. It couldn't get any better than this. It couldn't. Her nails raked down to his buttocks as she tried to shift his weight, to bring him fully over her, fully in her.

"Easy, sweetheart. Easy." Quinn kept his arousal tight against her but did not lift his lower body over hers. He knew if he did what restraint he had would crumble. He looked into her eyes then, eyes silvered bright with desire. "Lie back. Let me love you. I want you to go the distance, Emmi."

His steady hand moved from her breast downward, first warming the length of her leg to her knee before starting upward to stroke the soft skin of her inner thigh. Emily tensed when he bent her knee and coaxed her legs open. She heard the low rumble of his words in her ear, love words to soothe and calm her as he cupped and caressed her at the hot joining point of her thighs. His touch, exquisitely light, fired new, unfamiliar responses, a deep foreign throb that left her at once filled and empty.

When she writhed under his hand, Quinn's silky finger stayed with her, dipping inward. He withdrew it with a shivery slowness, then entered again. Emily arched to his hand, choking out tiny cries, half growl, half purr. In her heat and moisture, his fingers sensed her need and he groaned. His own desire was now a solid pound in his groin, but still he stroked her.

Emily was a wild thing. Her hands tore at the sheets, then his shoulders. Her long-denied body screamed for the release only he could give her. She reached for him, stroked him, her plea silent but sexually eloquent. When her hand curled around his erection, Quinn's groan was low and harsh. He added a silent curse when he left her to protect them, returning quickly to settle himself between her open thighs. When he kissed her, she took his tongue deep into her mouth and lifted herself to him. He entered her then, and she closed around him. When he filled her, he stopped, letting her adjust to him. He wasn't a small man. He heard a muffled cry and pulled back. Had he hurt her?

"Don't stop," she moaned. "Don't ever stop." She rocked her pelvis upward.

"You feel good, Emily. So hot—" *And tight*, he added to himself. *So incredibly tight*. He thrust deep and long, working to govern himself, to please her fully. His breathing was short and shallow, his control in tatters. When Emily started to cry out and squirm against him, he was lost. He was hard, hot, a primal male with instincts honed by nature and experience, and he bowed to them, giving her long, potent strokes. He heard his own plea.

"Stay with me, Emmi," he cried. "Come to me."

His mouth found the taut bud of her now-glistening

breast and took it, sucking hard in tandem with his forceful thrusts.

Emily was burning from the inside out, hurting, wanting, reaching. Her body quivered and shook and she arched into him.

"Quinn," she gasped, her fingernails raking his naked back as she clawed him closer. She closed tight around his length, giving way to her own body's spasm.

Quinn held himself still, his damp body trembling with the effort. It was worth it. She climaxed under him with shattering intensity. He had never experienced anything like it, the pulsing waves, the strength of her inner convulsions. His Emily. With a groan, he cupped her buttocks, lifted her to him, and plunged deep, then deeper again, his own release as powerful as hers.

For a long while, they clung to each other, letting their overheated bodies adapt to a cooler, quieter world. When Quinn rolled away from her, Emily felt an instant chill. He reached across her to drag the edge of the bedspread over her naked back, then pulled her to him.

Quinn looked down at the woman snuggled into his chest. Her eyes were closed, and he enjoyed watching her openly without interruption. He liked the tiny pleased smile playing across her lips. She opened her eyes, those mysterious rain-colored eyes, and gave him a look so intense, so filled with satisfaction he thought his heart would break from his chest.

"I didn't know," she closed her eyes for a brief moment. "I didn't know it could be like that. So . . . so intense, so cataclysmic."

"It isn't always, you know." He trailed a finger down her cheek. "We're good together. Better than good."

"It was . . . okay for you then?"

"Okay! It was spectacular. You're a wonderful

lover, Emily." He put his mouth to her ear, deepening his voice to a teasing whisper. "Very, very hot," he added, taking a small bite of her lobe.

"I think it has something to do with the coach."

"The coach had very little to do with it. You're a natural."

She smiled then. "I knew there had to be a sport I was good at." Emily stretched, a full languid stretch, and Quinn watched the movement of her breasts. He couldn't resist kissing each pert nipple. She shuddered and smiled into his eyes.

"Do you have any idea what that feels like? How you make me feel?"

He propped his head up on one hand and his expression turned serious. "I can only guess. Tell me, Emmi. Tell me how I make you feel."

"You make me feel like a woman. Whole and new. Like Eve. A woman for the first time. When you touch me, I can't breathe. I go crazy like . . . ," she closed her eyes for the image, "a high-tension wire cut in a storm, thrashing and sparking in a wet city street. It's odd, but when you kiss my breast, like you did then, I feel it . . ." She glanced up at him, saw his grin, and blushed. "I think you know where I feel it," she finished.

"I think I do."

She touched a finger to his lips and asked, "Why are you smiling like that? Or do you just like to see me turn red and squirm?"

"I'm smiling because you make me happy. But I admit I also like it when you squirm. Especially under me. I like that a lot." His grin broadened and Emily laughed. She didn't want to be shy and reticent, not after what they'd shared. For the time she had him, Quinn was going to have a full woman, no fears, no panics, and no regrets. She loved him so much. She was filled with it. With no warning her eyes filled with tears. She closed them but not soon enough.

"Emily. Love. What's the matter?" Quinn's voice was filled with concern.

"Nothing," she lied. He didn't look convinced. "I guess I find making love a bit overwhelming—find you a bit overwhelming." That part was close to the truth anyway. She remembered reading that somewhere. If you have to lie, incorporate as much truth as possible; it will be more believable.

Quinn gazed at her, uncertain whether to believe her or not. "You're a bit overwhelming yourself, Emily Welland. As a matter of fact, a *lot* overwhelming."

Emily watched his sober expression a second or two before speaking. There was so much she wanted to say, so much to leave unsaid. She searched for safe ground and found it as she gazed at him. "I love your eyes. Did you know that? They're the color of the ocean during a twilight storm. Such a dark, moody blue." She ran a curious finger along the line of his eyebrow and down his cheek, delighting in the freedom to touch and stroke him. Quinn turned his head and caught the finger in his mouth, biting gently before turning her palm to his mouth for a kiss. The long, seductive look he gave her stopped her breathing.

"With all those pretty words, you could turn a man's head." *One hundred and eighty degrees*, he thought to himself, but it was too soon to tell her that. *A few more days. Just a few more days.* "Now what about that dinner and hotel room waiting for us in Victoria?"

Emily snuggled closer and ran a hand across his chest. "What about it?" Her hand slipped lower.

With iron will he stopped her exploration. "No, you don't. One more inch and I'll never see your hometown.'' He leaned over to give her a light kiss. When she started to deepen the kiss, he pulled back, took a short breath, and smiled. ''You don't exactly play fair, do you? Are you trying to tell me you've lost interest in going to Victoria?''

Emily threw herself back on the bed. She knew Quinn wanted to see Victoria. It had been he who'd made all the arrangements. She was being selfish. He was on a holiday, after all, with only three weeks left. She sat up then and grinned at him. ''All right. Victoria it is. If we hurry, we can make the next ferry.''

He grinned and kissed her again before turning to sit on the edge of the bed. When he turned his back to her, she cried out, ''Quinn! Your back!'' Emily's hand flew to her mouth. Had she done that?

''What's the matter?''

''Your back, it's . . . scratched.''

''I expected it would be. Don't worry about it.'' He smiled at her. ''I'm not too proud to wear a few scars. Quite the opposite in fact.''

Emily was stunned. She still couldn't believe she had done it. My God, a couple of the scratches were deep, even bleeding slightly. She was mortified. She resolved then and there to give her long nails a severe trimming.

''I must have . . . hurt you. I'm so sorry.'' Emily was sitting in the middle of the bed with the cover pulled to her chin. She was bright pink and plainly miserable.

When Quinn threw his head back and laughed, Emily blushed deeper and cast her eyes downward. He took her face in his hands. ''Emmi, stop worrying. A few scratches won't hurt me. It happens. Not often enough, actually. I'll probably walk around for the next few weeks with my shirt off just to show them off,'' he finished, grinning at her.

"You wouldn't!"

"Why not?" he teased.

"I'd die. That's why. Promise me you won't take your shirt off until they're gone. Promise me, Quinn, please!"

"You mean you don't want everyone on Salt Spring to know you're a long-nailed tigress in bed? That in the heat of passion you tore me apart?"

"I want only you to know that, and if you don't keep your shirt on, I will tear you apart." Emily was smiling now, but the threat sounded real. "Promise? You'll keep your shirt on. No matter what?"

"I promise," he said solemnly and crossed his heart. "I'll keep it on the rest of my life if you promise to scratch me some more." He reached for her then and pulled the cover down to expose her breasts. *Damn Victoria*, he thought.

Emily leaped back. "No way. We've got a ferry to catch, remember." She pulled the cover back up.

Quinn cocked his head as if to deliberate, then smiled. "Right. But let's finish where we started . . . in the shower." He offered a hand to pull her from the bed. "But you have to promise to be careful with me, I am, after all, a wounded man."

They missed the next ferry but managed to catch the one after that.

NINE

If you ever want to appreciate your hometown, see it through the eyes of a tourist, Emily thought. It was the following Wednesday afternoon, and as she stood with Quinn's arms around her on the foredeck of the ferry taking them back to Salt Spring, she brimmed with happiness and new precious memories of Quinn and the town she had grown up in. From now on they would be inexorably linked. The weather had obliged, and Victoria, dressed as always in Olde England ambience, was vivid with flowers and sunshine.

They had covered most of it on foot, touring the circumference of the Inner Harbour, ambling along newly restored Government Street with its trendy shops, then to the Parliament buildings, the Provincial Museum, and the Undersea Gardens. She discovered that Quinn was an interested and determined tourist. In three days, he knew more about Victoria than she did. Before, she had seen it only as home. Now it was a romantic city filled with charm and priceless remembrances. Sighing deeply, she leaned her head back against his shoulder and pulled his arms tighter around her. In minutes they would be docking.

Quinn gladly tightened his grip on her. He heard her sigh and asked, "What's going on in that head of yours? Glad to be getting home?"

"I'm always happy to see the island, but that wasn't what was in my mind. I was pasting pictures in my album."

"You didn't take any pictures."

"Oh, yes, I did. Hundreds of them. And they're all right up here." Emily touched her head.

He smiled into her hair. "Did you take one at Beaver Lake?"

She turned in his arms and her grin was infectious. "That one goes in a separate album. One with three X's on the cover."

"That good, huh?"

"That good." She reached a hand up to caress the dark curls at his nape.

She wondered if he'd planned it. She would never know, and it didn't matter. What mattered was that he'd made the most incredible love to her—there, at the lake, where her panic and fears had taken root that night so long ago. Thinking about their lovemaking, Emily dropped her eyes. They'd acted like a pair of teenagers, laughing at their own clumsy efforts to find a comfortable position in the Rover. Emily felt a growing heat when she thought about it. Quinn had been most ingenious! When she teased him about it afterward, telling him he must have done a lot of parking in his time, he'd laughed. An inescapable part of coming of age in California, he'd said, practically a rite of passage even for late starters like him. Emily believed him.

The slight bump of the ferry against the dock reminded them it was time to get back in the car. Reluctantly, Emily left his arms.

"We're home," she said without thinking.

She didn't notice Quinn's happy nod.

He dropped her off at her place and carried her bag inside. "What time is the dress rehearsal?"

"Eight o'clock."

He pulled her close. "Shall I pick you up?"

"No. I'll meet you there. I'll probably go early. I want to see one of the sets they finished yesterday. Besides, there's no reason for you to drive all the way here to get me. The hall is only minutes from where you're staying." She stood on tiptoe and brushed a kiss across his lips. "I'll see you there. Okay?"

"Okay." Not content with her gentle kiss, Quinn crushed her to him and deepened it. His voice was husky when he lifted his head. "Four whole hours without you. I'm not sure I can stand it." He gave her a last hug and a sexily suggestive smile and was gone.

Emily stood in the open doorway and watched him go. *Seventeen more days*, she said to herself. *I have him for seventeen more days*. When the thought of his leaving brought down a dark curtain of depression, she fought it. *The cup is half full*, she told herself, *not half empty*. Fixing on happier thoughts, she headed over to Lynn's to pick up Bailly.

"Why so worried, Emmi? It wasn't that bad." Quinn went to the bar and poured them both a glass of wine. He'd insisted she come to his place after the dress rehearsal. By the look on her face she should be drinking straight scotch, not sipping white wine.

"Not bad! It was a disaster! We open in three days. They'll never get that set right by then. It's all wrong.

I should have done it myself. It's my fault. All my fault."

He handed her the glass of wine. "It will be okay. You'll work it out. You have to admit it was kind of funny." He struggled to keep his lips from twitching.

"Quinn Ramsay, if you laugh, you're a dead man."

He raised a hand and nodded, fixing what he hoped was an appropriately concerned expression on his face.

Emily glared at him. "Your eyes are still laughing," she accused.

"Come on, Emmi, they'll fix it. By Saturday there's no way that balloon will come down."

"It isn't only that it came down. It didn't even look like a balloon when it was up. And they won't fix it— I'll fix it." Emily ran a determined hand through her long hair. "The woman, Christine, is supposed to be up in the sky in a bright red balloon. That's what the play is about, her overcoming fear and embracing life. The balloon represents her fear. By going up in it, she takes the necessary risk and discovers that she's had the courage all along. The bloody balloon is crucial. The way they've done it, it looks like she's camping in the Ozarks. She looks like she's in a tent, a tent that collapses in the middle of the final scene, I might add." Emily took a long, nervous sip of wine. "There's my heroine saying her final stirring words wrapped in a shroud of cheap purple nylon. It isn't even the right color for heaven's sake. The script says red, not purple."

Quinn sat across from her on the love seat. He knew how much this play meant to her, and he was sorry to see her so disappointed. He had no idea how to comfort her.

As she sat staring morosely into her glass, he saw

her lips crease into an unwilling smile. He watched it grow.

"It was kind of funny, wasn't it?" she asked.

Quinn stayed silent. He didn't want to be a dead man. He wanted to stay very much alive and in Emily's good graces. He watched her pull back from her sour mood.

"And the look on my Christine's face. It would have done a horror queen proud. You'd have thought the building was falling in on her instead of a few yards of nylon. And the way she thrashed around . . . 'Get me out of here, get me out of here.' " Emily mimicked the unlucky actress before breaking into full-throated laughter. When she finally stopped, she glanced at Quinn. "Tell me, do you think this ruins my chances for a New York opening?" She laughed again. This time he joined her.

"It's going to be all right. You'll see. Until the balloon took a dive, the play was great. It was both funny and touching. That's a tough combination. You're a talented woman. And about that New York opening, if that was what you were aiming for, you'd be a shoo-in."

Emily stared at him, pleased with his praise and ecstatic at the confidence he had in her. Whatever would she do when he was gone? She had to let him know how she felt but didn't know how to do it without giving him the burden of her love. That she would not do.

She gave him a level gray gaze and looked for the right words. "You're an exceptional man. Did you know that? Today, the time in Victoria. I'll always remember it. I'm going to keep it—and you—here," she touched her heart, "always." She smiled then. "You're my very own red balloon."

When he started to get up from the love seat and move toward her, she raised a hand to stop him. "No. Don't come closer. If you do, I won't be able to string three coherent sentences together, and it's important I say what I'm going to say."

She paused, looking inside to find the right words, knowing she needed only three. Three short words she could not, would not, say. "What I said . . . about your being my red balloon . . . that's true. Being with you, making love with you has changed my life. I want you to know that. I'm never going to be the same. Maybe, just maybe, shy, fearful Emily Welland is gone forever. I will be grateful always. And when you leave, when you go back to your *real* life, I'm going to remember you with . . . special affection, very special affection."

Quinn was beside her now, blue eyes dark and strangely sad. "Affection? That's what you feel for me?"

Under the intensity of his gaze, she dropped her eyes. "Of course. What more could there be?"

"And when I leave? Go back to my *real* life? What will you feel then?"

"I will be sad you are going. I will miss you and I will, uh, wish you well." Her words were awkward and stilted.

Quinn got up and walked to the open patio doors. He took a deep pull of cool night air in an effort to ease the pressure building in his chest. Affection. The word stung. Had he misjudged what was between them? Were his own strong feelings blinding him to hers? *You've been a fool, Ramsay, a callous, unthinking fool—not to mention a hopeless romantic. Because she responded to you in bed doesn't mean she loves you, doesn't mean she wants to plan her life around you.*

He turned to look at her and saw the questioning, uneasy expression on her face. He knew, despite her brave words, shy Emily wasn't gone. She had broken the physical barrier, but the emotional one was still intact. *Time and patience*, he said to himself, moving back to her. He hoped he had enough of both to bring this woman to his heart with the same passion she'd come to his bed. One thing was certain, he wasn't giving up. He smiled when he reached her, hoping she wouldn't sense the false confidence at its root.

He stood over her a moment before bending to take her hands. She raised her eyes to meet his.

"Come here," he ordered, pulling her up and against the taut wall of his chest. He kissed her softly in a way he had never kissed her before. When she pulled away to give him a wondering gaze, he answered her unspoken question. "That was a thank you kiss. For letting me be your red balloon, and," he kissed her again, "for letting me change your life." For a brief moment, he held her away from him and his expression was serious. "The magic word is 'let,' Emmi. Remember that. It was you who made the decision, took the risk. It was the right time. You knew it and you acted on it. It's important you remember that. As for my part . . . ," he grinned, "you might say I rose to the occasion. Which I'm prepared to do right now if you think the time is right."

"Any time is the right time with you, Quinn."

He rested his forehead against hers. "You're damned good for the ego, darlin'. Did you know that?" His hands slipped beneath her shirt, then under the waistband of her jeans. She held her breath to give him room as his hands barely found space between fabric and flesh to grasp her buttocks and pull her firmly against him. "And you feel so good. I can't keep my hands off you."

"So? Who asked you to?" She nestled against him as his deft fingers undid the back of her bra. She closed her eyes when he took possession of her breasts and started to work his magic on her nipples. Her throat constricted and she swallowed, willing her rubbery legs to hold her. It didn't work. When they weakened, she clasped her hands behind his head.

"Emily?"

His voice was a soft breath in her ear.

"Hm, mm?"

Still caressing her breasts, he pulled his head back to look at her. "Look at me." Her eyes were smoky with desire. Her expression was so transfixed he wondered if she was even seeing him, but he had to go on, had to prepare her.

"I want you to think about something. Think about what you would do if I asked you for more . . . more than affection. Will you do that?" He continued to thumb her nipples and wondered if he was being quite fair, but he didn't want to do anything to change that look on her face. "Emmi," he prodded, "will you do that?"

"Uh-huh," she agreed, her hands palming their way under his shirt.

Her absent-minded answer didn't make him happy, but his own control was slipping fast. He sighed. Time enough for conversation later. She would stay the night, and they would talk. He would make her understand she could trust him and that what he felt for her was more, much more, than affection.

It didn't work out that way.

When Quinn woke a few hours later, he reached for her but she wasn't there. The clock said 4:12 A.M.

Instantly awake and just as instantly angry, he sat up and switched on the bedside lamp. It was then he saw the note.

> Quinn. See you tomorrow. Felt uncomfortable staying. Zach and Blanche and all. Also meant to tell you, I have to work the next couple of days. Marsha's mom is sick. Come by the bookstore?
>
> Emily

Quinn stared at the note, trying to come to terms with his growing frustration and sense of abandonment. How could she walk out and not tell him? Who cares what Zach and Blanche would think, anyway? He wanted her here. He threw his legs over the side of the bed and grabbed for his underwear. He stopped himself as he was pulling on his jeans. He was actually thinking of going after her. *Stupid fool*, he muttered, heading for the kitchen instead. He was still angry and tense.

Who the hell did she think she was walking out on him like that? So much for his plans to talk to her. An unbidden, unwelcome thought chastened him. He stood up from the fridge, milk container in hand, and headed for the darkened living room.

Sitting on the sofa, he rested his elbows on his knees, for now ignoring the milk container he dangled between them. He'd walked away from a few beds himself in his time. Without the courtesy of a note as he recalled. Until this moment he'd never realized how it made a person feel. Had the woman he'd left in bed experienced this aching sense of loneliness, this blunting of emotion as if the shared intimacy had no meaning or significance? *Not true*, he said to himself and stood up. He'd had genuine affection for those women. He started to drink and stopped abruptly, the milk carton frozen in the space near his lips.

Affection. That was the word Emily had used. After a wry smile, he took a drink of milk and wiped the back of his hand across his mouth. He understood now why she'd chosen that word.

"You're right, Emily," he said aloud. "It's easier to walk away from affection. Love is much more complicated."

He put the milk carton on the coffee table and went back to bed. He had a lot of thinking to do. He had a thousand ways to get a woman into his bed, but he had no idea how to keep one there. He'd never realized before they were two distinct talents. *I love you, Emily Welland*, he said to himself, *and I want you to love me*. He never wanted to hear the word "affection" again.

"Hi."

Emily looked up from what she was reading to see Quinn grinning at her and holding out a brown bag.

"Lunch?" He lifted the bag.

"I don't know. Did you make it, or did you press poor Blanche into duty?" She gave him a sidelong glance.

"What would you say if I told you I made it with my own two hands?"

Emily appeared to consider it. "I'd take a miss."

Quinn chuckled. "In that case, Blanche made it. How about it? We can go and sit on the same bench where I first looked into those rain-colored eyes of yours."

"Okay. But let me check with Grace first." Emily started from behind the counter.

"Not necessary." It was Grace. She was leaning in

the doorway between the shops. She nodded at Quinn and smiled. "I can manage fine. Go ahead and have your lunch. By the way, Em, I talked to Marsha. She says her mom is feeling better and to tell you she'll be back in on Friday."

"Great! With tonight and all day tomorrow the balloon should be ready on time." Emily felt the pressure ease. She'd probably be working all night, but at least now there was hope she would complete it. She stepped out from behind the counter.

Quinn put his arm around her shoulders and walked her to the door. When they turned back to say goodbye, Grace was watching them curiously. She glanced at Quinn. "Rain-colored eyes, eh? So that's what did it," she teased.

He didn't hesitate with his answer. "Yup. That's what did it."

"You wouldn't mind if I got contacts, would you, Emily? Gray ones?"

Emily smiled. "You make one move on this man, my friend, and you'd need more than contacts. I might just scratch your eyes out." Quinn's hand squeezed on her shoulder and he chuckled.

Grace giggled.

"I wouldn't laugh if I were you, Grace. I'll bet Emmi could be quite lethal with those nails of hers. If she had a mind to, that is." He smiled innocently.

Emily dragged him from the store.

In a couple of minutes they were across the street in Harbour Side Park. Quinn propped up his bike as she dug in the bag for their lunch.

"I'll go over there and get us some coffee," he said, nodding in the direction of a nearby restaurant.

Emily watched him go, enjoying the ripple of his muscular legs as he strode across the grass to the restaurant. He walked so purposefully, she thought, his masculine stride even and long. But then, everything about him was filled with purpose. That's why he's been so successful. He sees what he wants and goes for it. How she wished she could be like that. She thought how much she would miss him and quickly shoved the thought aside, directing all her energies to the here and now, refusing to think beyond that. She was living in a time warp, she knew that, a lover's time warp. But it was the safe way, the surest way, to avoid being hurt. Still, she did have a question to ask if for no other reason than to confirm she hadn't been dreaming.

"Here we are. And from a fresh pot. The heavens are tilted in our favor today." He was back. He handed her a coffee and took a drink from his own as he looked at her. "I missed you this morning."

"I missed you, too, but I thought it was best I go. I might as well keep what's left of my reputation for . . . later." She took a bite from the salmon sandwich.

"Yes. I guess you should." He gave her a strange look. "Is it true what you told Grace about the time needed to finish your balloon?"

"I'm afraid so. I started on it this morning when I got home. Thinking of a pattern, things like that. It's going to take longer than I thought. I wasn't planning on working this week. Now, having to man the store today, I'll have to make the balloon tonight. And to be honest, I'm more comfortable with a power saw than a sewing machine. At least it will give you a rest from my insatiable demands on your body."

"That kind of rest I don't need." He stroked her arm. "You're telling me I won't see you tonight?"

"I don't think so." Her answer was filled with regret. More so when she saw matching emotion in his eyes. Their time together was so short, but the play, the balloon were important. She sighed.

He pulled his hand back, and Emily looked at her arm fully expecting to see scorch marks.

"When do you think you'll be finished?" he asked.

"I *have* to be finished by early tomorrow night. Granger wants the theater empty of cast and crew no later than eight. It's a long-standing rule of his. No last-minute pressure the night before opening. He says everyone should relax the night before opening." She smiled. "I think he wants everyone to go home and practice deep breathing."

"I knew I liked this Granger guy. Come to my place when you're finished. We'll have a swim, dinner, and then do the deep breathing. What do you say?"

"I say yes. You are exactly what I need to keep my mind off opening night. And I can't think of anyone I'd rather breathe with."

For a time they sat in silence feeding the greedy gulls the remnants of their lunch. One of the things Emily loved most about Quinn was his easy silences. Remembering what he'd told her about his older parents and the quiet of their home made her think it was they who had given him this gift. As the silence grew, her question bubbled to the surface.

"Quinn, did you—?"

He stopped feeding the birds and looked at her. For the first time in days, she looked hesitant. "Did I what?" he prodded.

"Nothing. I was probably imagining things."

"I thought we were past the unfinished sentence phase of our relationship. What were you going to say?" He went back to feeding a bold spotted gull that had walked up and pecked demandingly at his sneaker.

"I was going to ask what you said last night before

we . . . when you were, you know, kissing me? I'm not certain you said anything but I thought—''

She *had* heard him. Until now he hadn't been sure. He shooed the gulls away and gave her his full attention. ''I asked you to think about the possibility of my asking more from you than just affection.''

An icy clamp forced her ribs together, tight and confining. She took a deep, calming breath and straightened her shoulders to loosen it. ''You're not happy with the way things are with us?'' The thought of his answer terrified her. She'd thought things were beautiful. What was wrong? What had she done—not done?

''Happy! I'm more than happy.''

''Then I don't understand.''

This is it, Quinn. Time to put your mouth where your heart is. He swung one leg across the seat of the picnic bench. Now straddling it, he took her hands in his. ''I want you to think about falling in love with me, shy Emily. I want to know if there's a chance you can love me the way I love you.'' His eyes bored into hers, direct and questioning.

Quinn loved her! It wasn't possible. It couldn't be. Loving was a forever word, and wasn't he leaving in less than three weeks? All of her efforts, all of her courage had been channeled into his time on the island. Could she think beyond that? Dare she believe she could satisfy this man—always? Her heart beat an uneven rhythm of fear and hope. She dropped her eyes and squeezed his big hands hard.

Quinn watched her pale face, saw the welling of old fears and insecurities. Damn, he'd spoken too soon. He reached out and stroked the skin of her cheek, wanting to ease her tension. She responded to his hand by leaning her face into it but didn't speak.

''It's okay, sweetheart. You don't have to say anything. As a matter of fact, right now, I'd prefer you didn't. I'm asking you to think on it. That's all. We'll talk Friday night after you've finished your balloon.'' He ran his thumb along her lower lip, which gave every indication of starting to tremble. ''It can't be that hard to think about my loving you, can it?''

What was hard was thinking about anything else. Emily tried to concentrate on the sea of red nylon that claimed her living room. Sighing, she picked up the needle, determined to finish the next two seams before she went to bed. It was two A.M.

''Damn it!'' It must have been the tenth time she punctured her finger tonight. She raised it to her mouth, sucked the blood away, and stood up. Bailly's ears flicked, and he eyed her hopefully as she moved to the window.

She looked down at him. ''You could have gone to your bed, you know. You don't have to stay here with me.''

Bailly lifted his head and thumped the floor a couple of times with his tail.

A tired smile crossed her face as she looked down at him. ''You up for some fresh air, old guy?''

He was on his feet.

''Let's go then. We'll go to the beach for a minute and ponder love and red balloons.'' Woman and dog walked in quiet companionship to the water's edge.

Emily knew she loved Quinn. She'd known for days now. She smiled inwardly, thinking perhaps she'd loved him since that day in her bookstore when he'd asked her why he made her afraid. Still a good question, she thought. Even after all they'd shared, the laughter, the incredible physical intimacies, his love aroused more anxiety than faith, more fear than hope. ''You make me sound like an alien life form.'' That's what he'd said the first night at his place, when she'd told him she never expected him to love her. He'd been right. That was exactly what she thought, what she still thought. He was a California man, a flash of golden, perfect male with a sunshine existence full of people and places as foreign to her as perennial orchids were to her northern garden.

No. She'd never expected him to love her. Now that he did, could she hope he would keep on loving her? Wouldn't it be better to keep things as they were? Safe.

She kicked a stone with her toe and stuffed her hands deep in the pockets of her jeans. "Safe!" She spit the word out like a rancid nut and lifted her chin.

"I love you, Quinn Ramsay. I admit it scares me, and I don't know if we have the chance of an icicle in L.A. but, dear God, I love you so much I ache with it."

She looked upward and a moonlit smile curved her lips. She had told the moon. Tomorrow night she would tell him. No more being safe.

"C'mon, Bailly. I've got a balloon to finish." *And one to fly*, she thought, the crinkle of a smile still on her face.

TEN

"I think it's going to work. What do you think?" Emily turned her head to Betsy, her doubtful leading lady, and Granger. The three of them looked up at the brilliant red nylon suspended out of sight above the stage.

"Lower it one more time," Granger replied, one hand stroking the day's growth of beard on his narrow chin.

"Okay, but I'm sure it will work." Emily went offstage, untied a series of ropes fastened to a post offstage, and carefully lowered the red nylon. Her red balloon came down perfectly. She took a minute to glance at her watch. It was late. Almost nine.

"Damn. That's good, Emily." Granger smiled and waved a hand. "Tie it back up."

He turned to Betsy. "Looks like the danger of your balloon crash is past, thanks to our creative playwright. And now, my people," he glanced at the remaining cast members, "to quote a famous late-night TV newsman, 'We are outta here.' You're ready, the set is ready, and tomorrow we're going to knock 'em dead. Have a relaxing evening, everybody. Now beat it.''

Within fifteen minutes, Emily was at Quinn's door, a casserole dish of lasagna tucked under her arm. She may be starting to trust his love, but her faith in his culinary skills was not so ready. Her heart pounded as she rang the ship's bell hanging by the front door. Tonight was going to be a special night, she thought, full of love, promises, and . . .

He answered the bell wearing wet swim trunks, a white towel around his neck, and a wide grin. His dripping hair was curled tight against his head. It was obvious he'd just left the pool. He wasted no time pulling her into his arms.

"I brought dinner," she said inanely, a little stunned by the warmth of his welcome.

"I missed you," he groused good-naturedly in her ear. "I hope that damned red balloon was worth it." He kissed her then, just enough to make her toes curl. "Was it?"

She smiled and couldn't dim the soft light in her eyes when she answered. "I'm not at all sure—now that you've reminded me what I've been missing."

When a drop of water from his wet hair fell on her cheek, Quinn took his eyes from hers and stroked it away with a rough thumb. "I'm making you wet. Come in."

He was making her a lot more than wet. He released her then, pulled her inside, and closed the door.

"I hope you like Italian. I brought lasagna." *Why am I so obsessed with food?* she moaned to herself. *I'm standing here with this incredible man in front of me all shiny and wet and I'm chattering about pasta.* She sighed.

He took the casserole dish from her shaky hands, put it on the hall table, and pulled her back to his arms. "I love Italian. But I love you more, Emily Welland. So much so, it scares the hell out of me."

"Scares you?" she parroted, drinking in the intensity in his eyes.

"What scares me is that you might not love me back. I want to know, *need to know*, how you feel."

"Here? Now? Standing in the hall?"

His smile held a trace of impatience. "Why not? Will your feelings be any different in the few minutes it will take us to walk to the living room?"

"Oh, Quinn, my feelings for you won't change—ever! Not in minutes. Not in years. You are the best . . . the most wonderful thing that's ever happened to me."

His voice softened as he urged her on. "Say it, Emmi. I want to hear you say it." His eyes trapped her.

"I—"

The discordant clang of the ship's bell at the door cut her off. It was followed immediately by the entrance of a darkly tanned, blond man laden with suitcases. Emily looked at the stranger, then back to the man holding her in his arms. Quinn shook his head in surprise when he recognized the newcomer.

"Paul! I, uh, wasn't expecting you. Not tonight anyway."

The man stopped in his tracks and stared at the two people with their arms linked around each other. An apologetic expression came over his face as he shrugged a suitcase down from his shoulder.

"Sorry, I guess I should have called. This is not good—not good at all." He glanced over his shoulder out the open door.

Quinn rallied and headed toward him to help with the bags. He even managed a tight smile. "Inconvenient maybe but not the end of the world as your expression seems to imply. It seems I have to keep reminding you that this is *your* house, after all. Emily, this is Paul Severns. My current landlord and *former* friend." The added jibe was for Paul's benefit. *When I get him alone, I'll kill him*, Quinn decided, with only half the good nature of his jest.

Emily glanced at Quinn before taking Paul's hand. Quinn was annoyed, but this man looked as if the sky was falling. Quinn's tease hadn't lightened his mood. When Paul looked into her eyes and smiled, the smile was distracted, and again he glanced behind him.

"Look, I really am sorry, buddy. I didn't know. If I had, I never would have—"

"What in hell's the matter with you, Severns?" Quinn had never seen his friend so agitated.

"Quinn, *caro mio*!" The woman flew into Quinn's arms either unaware of or purposely ignoring Emily's presence. "How wonderful to see you! It has been so long—too long," she purred.

Emily could only stare as Gina Manzoni grabbed the ends of the towel around Quinn's neck and pulled his mouth to hers. She gave him a lingering, possessive kiss. Emily sagged against the table that held her abandoned lasagna and gaped openly. She couldn't help herself.

The woman before her, almost exactly her height, was beyond beautiful. She was a Mediterranean stunner, a certified, authentic ten. Perfect hair, perfect eyes, perfect skin, and perfect figure. Emily glanced away only to see herself and Gina reflected in the hall mirror. Comparison was unavoidable. Emily felt her chest wall crumble. *God*, she thought, painfully mesmerized by the two images in the mirror, *I look like spare parts*. She wanted to weep.

Gina's mouth was on his before Quinn could react. Frozen by shock, he stood like a rain-drenched statue, his mouth yielding nothing to hers. When he felt the probe of her tongue, he clenched his eyelids to gain control and grasped the rose-tipped fingers gripping his towel. With exaggerated care, he unclasped her hands and moved her away from him, his face taut with anger. Gina had a pleased look on her face as he glanced at Emily. She looked as though she'd just come down hard on a crossbar. The curses in his head would have shocked a waterfront tavern. But he knew Gina would relish a good fight.

He remembered how amused he'd been when she'd first told him that fighting energized her, made her hot. How she enjoyed emotions bouncing around like thunder and lightning. At first he hadn't believed her, but he found out later she hadn't lied. There would be no fight, nothing that would allow Gina to gather strength. If he had to, he would explain to Emily later. He moaned inwardly at the thought of that conversation.

"Sorry, man. Really sorry." It was Paul again.

Quinn glared at him, then back at Gina. He forced a smile to his rigid lips. "You've nothing to be sorry for." He picked up Paul's suitcase and reached for Gina's. "I think it's about time we got out of this hall. You could both probably use a drink. I know I can." He kicked the door shut with unnecessary ferocity.

Emily leaned against the hall wall and let the three-some pass. If she could, she would have merged into it and happily disappeared. She delayed following them to the living room, wishing now she had taken the time to shower and change before coming. Never, absolutely never, had she been in the company of three more physically perfect human beings. She knew it shouldn't matter, appearances weren't everything, were in fact nothing at all, but she couldn't ignore the differences between them, these glorious sun-drenched people and a quiet island girl. They looked like magazine covers. Paul, so blond and tanned with that soft white cotton sweater draped casually over his shoulders, was perfect for GQ, while Quinn, in his wet swimsuit, with his sexy good looks and swim-curled hair, was definitely *Playgirl* material. Centerfold, she added, her eyes relishing his long, muscular frame. And Gina? Gina would look good on anything from *Life* magazine to a French postcard. Emily smoothed back her hair and grimaced. Despite her recent weight loss and new haircut, she felt fat, frumpy, and frazzled. Reluctantly, she followed them down the short hallway.

Once in the living room, Quinn went behind the bar. He opened a beer for Paul and poured a hefty shot of scotch for himself and red wine for Gina. Emily declined a drink with a silent shake of her head. When Quinn looked into her sober gray eyes, he felt a little sick. Gina would not be easy on her. At that thought, the dark-haired beauty spoke.

"You have not introduced us, Quinn." She turned her earth-brown eyes to Emily for the first time.

"This is Emily Welland, Gina. Emily, I think you know who this is."

"Of course. I've seen your pictures, Miss Manzoni. They don't do you justice." Emily swallowed and worked to ignore the nervous fluttering in her stomach. At the first opportunity, she would make an exit.

"Call me Gina, please." She gave Emily a narrow, appraising look. When she started to speak again, Paul interrupted.

"You live on the island, Emily?" His smile was friendly and open. The fluttering lost its edge.

"Yes, I do. For about six years now."

"What in heaven's name do you do in such a remote area? Does it not get boring?" Gina interjected.

Remote area! Emily wanted to tell her that she lived within an hour or two of a couple of million people but decided against it. It wasn't her job to educate Gina Manzoni. Besides, to her it probably was *remote*.

"It's quiet . . . and peaceful but not boring. The people here are wonderful and my store keeps me busy." Emily couldn't remember the last time she was bored.

Paul spoke again. "What store is that, Emily?"

"I own a bookstore."

Gina moved to a chair near Quinn and sat down. "A bookstore!" she said as though Emily had told her she took in washing for a living. "And to you this is *interesting*?"

"Gina!" Quinn growled. "Stuff it!"

Paul ignored Quinn and Gina to concentrate on Emily. He seemed to accept that he couldn't do anything about the situation he'd created by bringing Gina with him and was obviously trying to make the best of it. "I've probably been in your place then. Is it in Ganges?"

Emily nodded. The fluttering was back but there was something else, too. A quick tightening in her spine. She decided she didn't like Gina Manzoni. Not one bit. Nor was she going to be intimidated by her. She straightened her shoulders to answer Paul's question. "If you have been in, I don't remember, and I think I would. The whole island knows about you." Emily gave Paul Severns her full attention. He was an attractive man. She would have remembered those bright blue eyes and blond hair. She would have remembered the feeling of empathy that he exuded. "Maybe you went to my competitor," she added with a shy smile.

"Maybe I did. If so, I won't make the same mistake again. I'm sure your competitor isn't half as lovely as you." He grinned at her then and she smiled back. Was he flirting with her?

Quinn glowered at his friend. It was definite. Paul was in major trouble. First Gina rides in on his coattails and then he makes moves on Emily. "Emily is a writer, too. Her first play is being staged tomorrow night." He decided he'd better join this conversation before it got right out of hand.

"Great! Why don't we all go? I'd like to see what you've done. Tell us about it," Paul said with genuine enthusiasm.

Emily paled, then reddened. Her distraught expression told Quinn he'd made a serious error.

"No! That wouldn't be a good idea at all." Emily turned beseeching eyes toward Quinn. Why, oh why, had he brought up her play? These people were professionals. They would laugh at her paltry effort. "I'm sure my play wouldn't interest you at all."

Gina smiled. "Oh, but we would love to come. All of us. Would we not, Quinn? It will be . . . fascinating." Gina's agreement was too fast, too easy. Quinn studied her over the rim of his glass. What was she up to?

"Really, you wouldn't like it. I mean, it's amateur stuff. It's nice of you but—" She was desperate to convince them not to come.

Paul broke in. "No buts. We're coming and that's that. I got my start in amateur theater. It's been a long time since I've had the chance to enjoy it. It will be perfect." His eagerness was genuine.

"Yes. *Perfetto*." Gina echoed quietly, appearing to relish the other woman's discomfort. Emily looked as though someone had put matches under her fingernails. Gina decided to light one. "You are afraid we'll upstage you, *cara*?"

"Upstage?"

"It is opening night. Is it not? Perhaps you are afraid we steal your limelight? If that is how you feel, we will understand. We are all in the same business . . . in a way. *Si*?" Gina paused for dramatic effect. "Or is there another reason you do not want us to come to your, uh, *little* production?"

Being upstaged was the last thought on Emily's mind. Or at least she thought it was. Gina's tone irritated her and she sensed the challenge in her words. She was saved from answering by Paul's sharp interjection.

"Don't be so patronizing, Gina. Emily just has a case of opening night jitters. You've never worked in live theater, so you wouldn't understand that. But maybe we have been insensitive. Correction, *I've* been insensitive. If you don't want us to come, Emily, we won't. Say the word."

"I will be . . . pleased if you would come." Emily reached through her self-doubt and grabbed her pride. She had nothing to be ashamed of. Least of all her play. "I didn't mean to sound . . . inhospitable."

"It is settled then." Gina looked pleased as she tossed a look in Emily's direction. "Now tell me, *cara*, what does one wear to an opening night on . . . where are we again, Paul?"

"Gina!" He spoke the name with a roll of his eyes.

"Oh, yes, Salt Spring Island?" She appraised Emily's outfit of jeans and a T-shirt with undisguised scorn. "I would not want to . . . how do you say? . . . *overdress* for the occasion."

Emily's shoulders stiffened at the implied criticism. "Whatever you choose to wear will be fine. We're very casual on the island."

"Yes, that I can see," she drawled. "Comfort before fashion, *si*?"

Emily turned her silver eyes directly to the woman across from her. This time she looked *in*, not *at*, her, and this time the comparison was not so painful. Gina's almond eyes were callous, hard, and without hesitancy. Everything about her spoke of aggressiveness, ambition, and self-concern. This was the woman Quinn had loved, come close to marrying? A woman so different from herself—so forceful? She couldn't imagine it, but it was true. How many more people like Gina populated his world? It didn't bear thinking about. No. She was wrong. It did bear thinking about, a great deal of thinking. This was her first honest glimpse of his world. From what she could see, she would be as much at home there as on Pluto. A curl of misery and confusion twisted through her core.

Quinn watched the exchange between the two women with interest. He couldn't help but compare them. He also couldn't help patting himself on the back for the choice he'd made. Whatever fate had brought him to this island, to Emily, he didn't know, but he would be forever grateful. He was relieved when Emily invited Paul and Gina to her opening. She had every reason to be proud of her play. He knew Paul would love it. As for Gina . . . He shrugged inwardly. It simply didn't matter.

Emily's sudden rise to her feet caught him off guard. "If you'll excuse me, I think I'll head home. It's been a long day, and I have a dog to see to. I'm sure the three of you have a lot of catching up to do."

"Miss Manzoni." Emily nodded in Gina's direction.

'Paul stood up and took her hand. "Until tomorrow then. It was nice meeting you, Emily—real nice."

Emily smiled. She liked Paul Severns. He made her a bit uneasy, but she liked him.

Quinn frowned at his friend. It actually looked as if he was going to kiss her hand. His voice was gruff when he spoke. "I'll walk you to your car, Emmi."

Emily looked at his stern face. He looked angry and all too anxious for her to leave. She was silent as he took her arm and walked her to the door.

"I'm sorry about tonight. I had no idea Paul would arrive today, and Gina . . . well she was a complete surprise. You don't mind too much, do you?" They were at her car now, and he pulled her into his arms. "I'll visit for a while and then come over to your place. We can finish what we started before the arrival of my, uh, guests." He kissed her throat, that special place under her ear, and Emily felt her senses quicken. She pushed him away.

"No. Don't do that," she said too quickly.

He gave her a puzzled look. "Why not?"

"It would be . . . rude. Yes. Rude. They're your friends. You can't walk out on them."

"Only one of them is a *friend*, and he would be the first one to understand. Give me an hour and I'll be over." He was holding her loosely about the waist.

"No. Please, Quinn. Not tonight."

He dropped his arms and gave her an intent look.

She looked away from him.

"It's Gina, isn't it? I told you. What was between us is over."

"I know. I can feel it." She raised sad eyes to his. *And I'm beginning to feel how wrong I am for you, Quinn Ramsay, and it makes my soul ache.*

"What is it then?"

"I need to think, that's all. Before—"

"Before what?" he demanded.

"Before I make the worst mistake of *your* life." She looked away then. "Oh, Quinn, you're so different from me. Until tonight, I guess I'd forgotten how different. Meeting your friends was a reminder. You're all . . . so confident, so sure of yourselves, what you want, how to get it. To you, everything seems possible. Your life, your world, is so much larger than mine and so . . . at odds with it. It makes me afraid."

His throat constricted. "You have nothing to be afraid of. Don't you know that by now? I love you. I love you enough to erase those fears. You have to believe that."

"I can't," she stated simply. "Much as I might want to, I can't."

Before he could answer her, she took his face in her hands and pulled it to her own. She met no resistance as his lips slanted over hers. His hot tongue swept over her lips into the warmth of her mouth. Emily clung to the kiss as though it were a waking dream.

He heard her sigh his name against his lips as she pulled away and gazed up at him. "Good night, Quinn. See you tomorrow." She left his arms and got into her car. Once settled, she looked back at him from the car window, her look questioning.

"You won't forget that James races tomorrow, will you? You wouldn't disappoint him?"

"Of course not!" His tone was angrier than he intended, but damn it, she knew he wouldn't miss seeing James run. Certainly not on his *guests'* account. "I'll pick you up. We'll take the ferry together."

"You don't have to do that. I'll catch a ride with Grace and her parents. They're going over in her dad's powerboat. I'll see you there. Okay?" She knew Quinn would be welcome to ride with them, but she didn't offer the invitation. It was time for distance, a time for winding down the relationship.

He didn't answer. What was wrong with her? This evening had ended up a long way from where he'd planned.

"Okay?" she repeated when he didn't answer.

"Yeah. Okay. See you at the race."

His frustration grew as he watched her reverse up the long driveway. He felt . . . cut loose. As though Emily had silently, gently slipped his moorings. Tomorrow. Tomorrow he would talk to her.

He shivered and realized he was still wearing his damp swim trunks. He needed to change. When he headed back to the house, his thoughts turned to Gina. How was he going to get rid of her? Damn Paul to hell and back. What had he been thinking of to bring her here?

Paul was alone in the living room when Quinn returned.

"You and I have to talk. Where's Gina?" Quinn barked.

Paul shrugged. "Doing whatever women do before they go to bed, I suppose. Have no doubt she'll be back. It's not easy to get rid of Gina." Paul's smile was forced as his expression once again turned contrite, or was it guilty? "I said I was sorry, buddy. I didn't want to bring her. You must know Gina is a woman adept at getting what she wants."

Quinn studied Paul's face for a long moment and then almost choked when the truth finally hit him. "What the hell! You're sleeping with her, aren't you? That's what this is all about."

When Paul didn't answer, Quinn spun around and headed to the bar. He was disgusted with himself, Paul, and Gina. It was like a bad farce with the three of them the dissolute stars. Emily was right. His world was at odds with hers, in ways she couldn't imagine. He couldn't wait to leave it behind.

"I'm sorry, Quinn. Honestly sorry." He raised his hands and shrugged. "I couldn't help it. She kind of got to me, I guess."

What Quinn saw in his friend's face then surprised him. He had to know. "You love her? You actually love her?" The question was laced with amazement.

For a moment, it looked as if Paul was going to deny it. Then he nodded.

"You poor bastard." Quinn took a long pull on his drink and slammed the glass on the bar. "If you don't mind, I think I'll leave you two lovebirds alone. I'll get a room in town."

"You don't have to do that," Paul protested.

"No, I don't. But I have no desire to lie awake tonight wondering which bed Gina Manzoni is going to crawl into."

Paul winced and nodded. He had no illusions since he'd watched Gina pounce on Quinn when they came in tonight. He'd been royally used and knew it.

Quinn stormed out of the room to pack. When he came back, Paul was still alone, nursing his drink. "How long are you planning to stay here?" he asked without preamble.

"Only a day or two. I'm heading for New York on Monday. Look, Quinn—" Paul stood as he spoke.

"Forget it. Now's not the time to talk. Any and all conversation between us at this point would risk a valued friendship." Quinn looked long and hard at his friend and shook his head in amazement. "Gina Manzoni! I can't damn well believe it. You need help, my man. Isn't there somewhere you can go? Maybe take a cure?''

He didn't wait for Paul's reply. Paul turned to the night view of the water as the door crashed closed behind his angry friend.

"You did it, James. You really did it! I'm so proud of you I could burst." Emily was hugging James, and although he was happy at her praise, he wriggled to free himself from her grasp.

"I was good, Emmi. Damn good," he crowed, fingering his first-place ribbon as if it was spun gold rather than cheap satin.

Emily smiled at his mild curse. He sounded like Quinn. She didn't know that very man was behind them until he spoke.

"That you were, James. And you're going to be even better next time out." He clapped his big hand on the boy's shoulder and grinned. "Well done, son. That was one hell of a race you ran. When I ran my first race, I managed only a second. But I can tell you one thing. No other race will be as sweet in victory."

Emily turned at the sound of Quinn's deep voice. It was the first time today that they'd been together. While she sat in the stands cheering with Grace and Lynn, he'd been on the field. The minute she'd turned to him, his eyes fixed on her face. Both of them were awkwardly silent.

"How about something cold to drink? I don't know about you two, but I'm doing a slow bake in this sun." Lynn fanned her chest with her T-shirt and put her arm around her son. She gave him yet another proud squeeze. "How about you, track star, want some lemonade?"

James grinned and nodded.

"I have to pass, Lynn. I think I'll try to catch the next ferry to the island." Now that James's race was over, Emily's thoughts were on her play. She wanted to be at the hall early, in case there were last-minute problems. She also wanted to get away from Quinn.

"Quinn, lemonade?" Lynn asked.

He started to say no but caught the hopeful look on James's face and decided it was too early to leave him. Besides, Emily didn't seem to expect him to go back with her. He'd never seen her act so cool, so composed. Again he had the feeling he'd been cut adrift. What he didn't understand was why.

"Sounds good. Besides, I can't resist basking a while longer in James's glory. I'll see you later, Emily. The play starts at eight, right?"

"Right."

"Shall I pick you up, or would you prefer to go in your own car?" His eyes waited for her answer.

"I'll, uh, take my own car. It will be better that way."

Better for whom? he wondered. "See you there then. And if I don't get a chance to say it before first curtain, break a leg." He was studiously nonchalant, and Emily felt a curious chill.

"Ditto from me, Em." Lynn gave her a hug. "I'm sorry I won't be there to see your triumph."

Emily smiled her good-bye and watched the three of them head for the lemonade. Quinn's arm was draped over James's shoulder, and the boy was talking a mile a minute. She was still standing in the same spot when Quinn turned to look back at her. She couldn't read his eyes. He gave her a casual wave and returned his attention to James.

A lump formed in Emily's throat and her eyes filled with tears. Tears of happiness for James's victory or tears of pain at her coming loss? She brushed them from her cheeks. Either way they were damp, useless things. She turned to go.

By seven o'clock the community hall was a madhouse. Emily could almost see the ragged nerves of the cast and crew, jumping and sparking behind the closed curtain. There were bad jokes everyone laughed at, world-class jitters, a few tears, and a lot of bravado. But most of all there was a united determination to put on a good show. It was exhilarating. There was little or nothing for Emily to do except help with makeup and listen to last-minute complaints about lines in the second act. She was in turn scared, elated, frenzied, and resigned. She'd never felt more creatively alive. Her play, her baby, was about to be born.

As curtain time approached, a hush fell over backstage. The cast could hear the house filling up and it quieted them. Emily looked up at her balloon and said a final prayer to whatever saint was in charge of theater sets. She resisted the temptation to look out at the audience to see if Quinn had arrived yet. Besides, Betsy Mason, her timid Christine, was doing enough looking for both of them.

"I can't believe it! It's not possible. Granger. Emily. Come here. Look who's in the audience." Betsy's voice rose to such a pitch that Granger shushed her, putting a firm finger to his own mouth.

"Keep it down. This is a small hall. They'll hear you—and come away from the curtain."

The threat of plague couldn't have pulled Betsy from that curtain. "That's Gina Manzoni! It is. It truly is. Oh, my God, I'll die if I have to act in front of her. Just die!" Betsy sagged against the curtain as Granger came up behind her. Emily watched them both with a sinking heart.

"Well, I'll be damned!" Granger muttered. "I'll just be damned. Who's the blond guy with her?"

"Paul Severns," Emily sighed in answer without bothering to look. Might as well get it over with.

"The director? The one who won an Oscar a couple of years back?" Granger sounded shell-shocked.

"The same," Emily answered.

"Oh, my God." Granger moved in for a closer look.

It seemed "oh, my God" was the response of choice by everyone on sight of the shining Hollywood couple. As more of the cast joined them at the curtain, the expression took on the aspect of a mantra. The most disturbing thing was that by simply showing up, Gina and Paul had turned the happily determined cast of players back into a disparate, very worried group of ferry workers, store clerks, and homemakers. Emily was powerless to change that . . . or was she?

Quietly, she got off the stool she was on and joined the throng at the curtain. She hoped her voice would carry over the continuing chorus of oh-my-Gods.

"Paul Severns started in amateur theater. Did you know that? He adores it. Goes all the time."

"He does?" Granger asked.

"Yup. Says the best talent in the world is in amateur theater. When he heard about the opening tonight, he couldn't wait to come. Gina too." Emily nearly lost it on that one.

"How do you know so much?" Betsy sounded skeptical.

"He told me. I had a drink with them last night. They're friends of Quinn Ramsay. You remember. The man who came to the dress rehearsal with me?" She prodded their memories. "I guess Quinn told them how good everyone was, so they decided to come."

The group was silent until Granger, after taking one last look out the curtain break, looked at his watch and started to speak.

"Well then, people, it looks like we have something to prove then. Right?" He gave a firm look to the nervous group and smiled. Emily could see them straighten under his gaze.

"Right," they chorused. Emily let out the air in her lungs. It was going to be all right.

"Let's take our places, shall we?" Granger continued. "It's four minutes to curtain."

As the group left, Emily stole a quick glance at the audience. Her eyes found Quinn instantly. He was standing to take off his jacket. She lapped him up. He was so tall, so . . . beautiful. How would it be without him? Hard, was the answer, very, very hard. She closed the curtain and for a moment clung to its pleats. The fabric lent no strength and she moved to the side of the stage. For the next couple of hours, she hoped that seeing her words come to life would help her forget her heart was dying.

Quinn settled back in his seat and eyed the curtain, wondering what Emily was doing back there. All he'd done since last night was wonder about her. Tonight he would find out what spooked her. She was the most skittery woman he'd ever known. What she needed, he thought, was some wins. Some real wins. Quinn knew from experience that winning was the greatest confidence builder there was. It was difficult to survive emotionally on losses. Trouble was, some people were so hard on themselves they didn't recognize the wins when they came along. He hoped Emily wasn't one of them.

He loved her and wanted her with an intensity that surprised him. She was fire in his heart and in his bed. He was determined to keep her in both.

Quinn rolled the short program in his hand and tapped it restlessly against his knee. Damn the woman. She was driving him crazy, but one thing was certain. Emily Welland wasn't going to kiss him off as easily as she thought. No way.

"Nervous?" It was Paul.

"A little. Emily is probably a wreck back there. I'm nervous for her."

"You need not worry, *carino*, this is not your . . . Broadway." Gina's tone was acid. She was sitting on the other side of Paul. Quinn had been careful to keep him between them. When he'd returned to the house for clothes, Gina had been waiting. Their fight had been monumental. Gina would have it no other way. It ended only when he told her he loved Emily and planned to marry her. Since then all that was between them was a frigid truce.

"It is to Emily, Gina," he finally answered, not bothering to look at her. "And if you think so little of it, why in hell did you come?"

Gina turned to Paul with a full, carefully developed smile. "Because it was important to Paul. What other reason could there be?" One olive-skinned hand stroked his arm.

Paul gave her a cool stare. "You're such a good actress, my sweet. Why is it I don't believe you?"

At that moment the curtain came up and all Quinn could think about was Emily's red balloon. Would everything go right for her? Already rigid with tension, he knew he would stay that way until Emmi's play was successfully over. It was the same feeling he'd had watching James race today. A tight, nervous expectancy edged with an alarming impotence. He had discovered something today. Being a concerned spectator took stamina. He wasn't sure he liked it.

By intermission, Quinn's program was in tatters. By the end of the play it was pulp. When Christine stepped into the shining red balloon and said her final lines, the pulp hit the floor, and he was on his feet along with the rest of the audience, an audience generous with applause and shouted praise. It was Paul who spoke first.

"She's talented, Quinn. Extremely so."

Quinn couldn't stop his grin from widening at Paul's praise. "Save those kind words for Emmi, Paul. You'll make her day. Coming from you, they'll make her whole damn year!"

"I mean every one of them. Can we go backstage?"

"I'd like to see anyone try to stop us. Come on." Quinn stepped into the narrow aisle.

"I go to the car. In case you are interested." Gina's tone was sarcastic as she stood to leave.

Quinn looked into Gina's stunningly beautiful face, spoiled now by an unappealing pout. By God, the woman was jealous, he realized. He suddenly felt a shot of pity for her. "You could come with us. It would please the cast," he suggested.

The invitation surprised her, and the pout evaporated, replaced by uncertainty.

"Paul?" She looked up with a question in her eyes.

"It would be a professional courtesy, Gina," he answered. "Why don't you light up that incredible face of yours with a *real* smile and come with us?" He offered her his arm, and Gina gave him a low, seductive laugh.

"*Vero?* That might be difficult, *carino*," she cooed,

then surprised the two men by looping her arms through theirs and smiling brightly. "Let us do it then. You two to the talented Emily. Me to lavish praise on the cast. I may be what you in America call a sore loser," she glanced up at Quinn, "but I do know how to act the star."

ELEVEN

Emily was in a state of stunned excitement, caught somewhere between relief that the play was over and a sort of elation paralysis. She sat sphinxlike as the backstage jubilation rolled toward her. Granger's voice came through first.

"A triumph! A full-scale bloody triumph! Did you hear them? I feel . . . absolutely, totally . . . delirious with pleasure. God, but I love the theater." His smile was big enough, deep enough to damage his face.

The cast and crew flowed toward her on a river of adrenaline, giving the dazed Emily no chance to respond. She wasn't at all sure she could if she tried. This time, this moment, was so incredibly precious, she wanted nothing but to savor it, hold it to her spirit. It deserved a moment or two of silence, but it wasn't to be.

As family and friends of the cast surged backstage the noise level tested the sound barrier. Awash in accolades, Emily moved away from the crush. When she looked back, she saw Quinn moving toward her. His smile was bigger than Granger's, and his eyes were bright with pride and pleasure. Without conscious thought, she went toward him. He wrapped her in his arms and rocked her.

"Emily, it was wonderful, truly wonderful. I'm so happy, so very proud for you." He hugged her hard and started to pull away. He wanted to look at her.

With no warning tears spilled from her eyes, and she clung to him, burying her face in his chest.

"I'm . . . so glad . . . you're here." She sniffed and sobbed the words.

"Where else would I be?"

"I . . . don't . . . know." Emily was clutching him with the tenacity of a kitten on a tree limb. Still choking out her words, she lifted her head and smiled. "I can't . . . stop . . . crying and I . . . don't understand. I'm so . . . happy." Emily knew she should pull away but she couldn't. This moment needed Quinn. She needed Quinn. Just a little longer, she promised herself as she pressed her body against his.

He cupped her chin and grinned into her tear-streaked face. "Tears of happiness. The best kind. Cry away, my darling. Cry away." He pulled her back to his heart.

Paul came up beside them. "The play was wonderful, Emily. You're a talented lady. If you can tear yourself away from this big guy, I'd like to hug you myself."

Emily turned and looked into a face filled with sincere admiration. "You mean that? You really liked it?"

Paul reached for her hands, pulled her forward, and gave her the promised hug. "I mean it. Any writer who can get people to laugh and sniffle a bit—in all the right places—is a true genius in my book. I loved it. And the cast was remarkable."

When Emily stepped back, she continued to hold his hands. "Will you tell them that? Praise from a professional, and such a famous one, would mean so much to them."

Paul responded to her earnest expression with a happy nod. "I'd be honored. Where do I start?"

Emily reclaimed her right hand and brushed away her tears. "With Granger. Let me introduce you. He'll be thrilled. Thank you so much." She lifted eyes, still silvered with tears, to Quinn. "Will you come, too?" She offered her free hand.

When a beaming Gina joined them, Emily introduced the California threesome to Granger, Betsy, and the rest of the players. She was right. They were thrilled. The visiting celebrities lent rare panache to a Salt Spring Island opening night. When Quinn saw Emily puzzling at Gina's open, friendly attitude, he took her hand and leaned down to whisper in her ear.

"Don't look so surprised, Emmi. Gina knows how to work a crowd, any crowd. It's her business, and these people are her paying customers. At least she hopes they'll be."

Emily nodded as though she understood, but Quinn could see she didn't. He couldn't imagine Emily "working" a crowd for any reason.

Emily looked at Gina through narrowed eyes. Wasn't this the same woman who was sneering at the production not twenty-four hours ago? How is it that she was able to adapt so easily to people? As Gina circulated through the buzzing throng, Emily studied the faces of the cast and crew. They were awestruck, bedazzled, and, yes, charmed by her.

Gina Manzoni was a chameleon, an adept chameleon. Emily visualized the tables being turned, with her trying to impress a strange crowd in L.A., Quinn's town. She shuddered at the thought. Even if she did manage not to faint from fear, she wouldn't handle it with one tenth of Gina's skill. As she continued to watch her, Emily felt a grudging admiration for the beautiful woman. She might not like her, but she wished she had half her poise and charisma. Quinn needed a woman with that kind of self-possession. Maybe they would get back together when he went home. Emily made a good effort to ignore the hot blast of jealousy that tore through her at the thought, although she was certain her nostrils flared. Compulsively, she gave Quinn's hand a possessive squeeze.

He squeezed back and looked down at her. "Tired?"

"Very."

He wrapped an arm around her. "Is there a cast party?"

"At Granger's," she said, cuddling closer to him. "Don't you want to go?"

"No, I don't think so."

"Want to go home?"

She nodded. Something in the way he asked brought moisture to her eyes. Emily Welland and Quinn Ramsay would never have a home. At least not one together.

After another flurry of congratulations and a round of good-byes, they were at the door. Paul and Gina were not far behind.

"Coming back to the house for a drink?" Paul asked, his arm around Gina's waist.

Gina was looking at Emily as though she'd never seen her before. There had been no exchange between the women all night, and now Emily forced her lips to smile when she caught the woman's studying look. She was glad to turn her eyes back to Quinn when he spoke.

"No. I don't think so, Paul. I'm going to take Emily home. I'll see you tomorrow."

"It's okay, Quinn. I have my car here. You go with your friends," Emily piped up.

Quinn's jaw tightened. She couldn't be certain but it looked as though he was grinding his teeth. She'd never seen him look so angry. His words, when he answered, were modulated to sound normal. "I said I'll see you home, Emily. I think we have a few things to discuss." His eyes, black under the pale light in the parking lot, brooked no argument. He turned to Paul. "What time are you two leaving?"

"I don't know. Around noon, I guess. Come for coffee before we go?" Paul asked.

"Yeah, sure. I'll be by around ten or so. Right after I check out of the hotel."

Hotel? Quinn was staying in a hotel? Emily looked at him curiously.

Quinn was leading Emily away when she heard Gina's low voice. The beautiful woman assessed Quinn boldly before turning to Emily.

"You are a lucky woman. He will make you a wonderful *marito*. If there was anything I could do to change that, I would. But," she shrugged, "as I cannot, *buono fortuna*." With that Gina turned to leave. Emily was thunderstruck when she hesitated, turned back to her again, and said, "Your play. It was good. Perhaps someday you will write beautiful words·for me."

Emily nodded her response and stayed in rapt silence until they reached Quinn's Rover. Gina's praise felt good, in an odd way more valuable than the other more effusive compliments she'd received tonight. Emily knew it had cost Gina to part with it.

"What's a *marito*?" she asked, taking a step up to the passenger seat of Quinn's jeep.

"A husband," he answered with authority while giving a lift to her elbow. God knows, that was one Italian word he knew. He'd heard it often enough. With no added comment, he closed the passenger door and walked around to the driver's side.

"What a strange remark."

Quinn turned the key in the ignition. "You think so?"

"Well, yes. What would possess her to say such a thing to me? I mean it's not as if we were—"

"Go on." Quinn tossed her a glance before turning the ATV onto Upper Ganges Road. "It's not as if we were what?"

"Were serious . . . or anything." Emily assumed Quinn would be embarrassed by Gina's thoughtless comment. She wanted to put him at ease, make sure he understood she had no illusions about their relationship. Yes, he'd said he loved her, but that was here— on Salt Spring. In his world their island love would live as long as pansies in the desert.

With a suddenness that surprised her, he jerked the car to the side of the road, slammed it into park, and glared at her. Then, with no preamble, he reached for her and pulled her hard into his arms. His mouth, at first angry and impatient, quickly softened to a seductive warmth. Emily fell into the heat of it and warmed her soul. Her arms slid to his neck, her fingers to his dark hair, and her heart to heaven. When his head moved to her throat, he took a deep breath. She wasn't sure she wanted him to speak. What she wanted was for him to hold her forever. But Quinn was determined to talk. Leaving one hand resting at the base of her throat, he leaned back against the door and looked at her.

The seriousness of his gaze made her squirm.

"Emmi, what's the matter?"

"Nothing. Nothing's the matter."

"Nothing! Is it nothing that's made you as skittery as a park squirrel since Paul and Gina arrived? I don't think so. Level with me. Tell me what's going on in that too busy, too smart head of yours."

Silence pressed itself between them. He waited, not taking his eyes off her.

"It's done between us, Quinn. It's . . . over." She blurted. "We need to say . . . good-bye."

Her words hit him like shrapnel. He was too stunned to answer.

Emily forged on. "We had an agreement. Remember?" She lifted her head in a show of strength. "You were going to help me with my, uh, problem and leave. No commitments. That's what you said, and that's what we agreed on."

"Maybe we did. But that was then and this is now. I love you, Emily. I haven't made any secret of that. And I think you love me, too."

"Island love, not real love. We got off track, that's all. This, uh, relationship of ours was about . . . sex, not love. We knew that from the beginning."

"You think what's between us is just sex?"

"Not 'just' sex . . . very good sex," she stammered miserably. This conversation wasn't going the way she intended. She couldn't think what to say to take the hurt from his face.

Quinn stared at her, his expression pained, then vacant. Without a word he started the vehicle and pulled back on the road. Did she truly believe their lovemaking could be reduced to "good sex"? He knew they were long past that. If he was truthful, he'd known from the first time he kissed her. Why the hell didn't she? He'd been so sure his own feelings were shared. He cursed himself for his own ego, but if she thought he was giving up, she was wrong. Stone cold dead wrong! What he needed was a plan, a surefire way to make Emily see how great they'd be—together. By taking one step, they could have something special, he was never more certain of anything in his life.

By the time they pulled into Emily's driveway, the air of silence between them was a bottleneck of confused thoughts, pained emotion, and unspoken words.

When Quinn stopped the car, he didn't bother to turn off the ignition. He didn't plan to stay and sure as hell didn't expect to get asked. It was Emily who turned the key. When the quiet of the night entered the car cab, she found her voice.

"I didn't mean that, Quinn. About it being only sex." She watched a muscle twitch in his jaw. She resisted touching it with a soothing finger. "I'm sorry if I hurt you."

"That's okay, Emily. It's nice to know I'm a satisfactory stud."

Emily looked stricken. "Oh, no! Please don't think that."

"What in hell am I supposed to think? And don't give me any of that affection crap."

"It's not that I don't care for you. I do. I tried to tell you that before Paul and Gina arrived. You've made a real difference in my life. You've . . . empowered me in a way I would never have believed possible. But even now, I can't—"

"Finish it. No more damned faltering. Say what you have to say and go in the house. Let's get this over with."

She looked at him, eyes pearlized with tears. "I can't make it in your world, Quinn. And you can't make it in mine." Emily dropped her eyes and rubbed her palms nervously against the top of her thighs.

Quinn stared at her long and hard but didn't speak as he considered her words. The beginning of hope unfurled near his heart, lending an uneasy calm to his next words. He cupped her face in his hand and claimed her eyes.

"Emmi, do you love me?" He watched, and when she tried to turn her head, he wouldn't let her.

"Answer me," he demanded gruffly.

"Yes! Yes, I love you! I love you so much I can't stand it. But what good is it? It would never work. I couldn't cope with your blindingly brilliant life-style, fast talk, fast cars, fast people. The pace is wrong for me. And you? Here? It's unthinkable. You'd go crazy. Don't you see how impossible it is?"

He raised two fingers to her lips. His heart was beating hard enough to break his ribs. She did love him. The rest was chopped liver. This was the opening he was looking for. His body said move. Get this woman where you can hold her.

"Let's take a walk."

In a second Emily's door was open and Quinn was dragging her into the moonlight.

They were on her beach, near the thinking log before he spoke again. Fighting for reason, Quinn pulled her against his long frame. "I did hear you right? You did say you love me?"

"I love you, Quinn Ramsay. And I won't do anything to ruin it." Emily saw the smoke in his heated gaze. She knew the fire wasn't far behind.

"Marry me," he demanded.

Emily gasped in surprise. "Marry you? Didn't you hear anything I said? We can't get married."

"Why not?"

"It would be like a marriage between two different life forms. That's why." She pulled herself from his arms.

"You mean all that crap about where we'll live." He gave her a probing look. "Ever hear of the word "compromise"? You're right, though. I couldn't live here, not right now anyway. But I love this island, and I would want—hell, I probably need—to come back to it for long periods and often. As for L.A., after I sell my business and get the foundation up and running, I don't need to live there. But for the next year or so, L.A. will be home base. In a business sense, I'm connected there, and those connections will be necessary to get the foundation well established. After that," he shrugged, "Seattle might be an option or maybe Portland."

"Foundation? I don't know what you're talking about." Emily's confusion showed clearly in her up-turned eyes.

"I would've told you sooner, but between your play, James's race, and my, uh, guests, the right time hasn't presented itself." He reached for a tendril of her hair, coiled it idly around his index finger, then dropped it. "Remember when you came to my place and I fed you burnt meat and a raw potato?"

When Emily nodded, Quinn moved toward her thinking log. He patted the empty spot beside him and she sat down.

"That night, you sensed I was worried about selling Action Sports because I had no concrete plan for the future." He leaned down, picked up a flat stone, and began flipping it in his hand like a coin. "Well, now I do. I guess you could say I owe it to James. The amount of pure heart he put into those games reminded me what sports are really all about. And today—seeing all those other kids, giving their best and more—well, it was just great. It was competition at its best, its purest. Every kid there was a winner. I'd forgotten that kind of dedication existed.'' He tossed the stone to the ocean and turned to her.

"I'm going to start a nonprofit sports foundation for physically and mentally challenged athletes. I think with some of my own funds plus what I can raise from my ex-competitors I could pull it off. I've already spoken to the main one, and he's all for it. The foundation would sponsor games, provide transportation and accomodation for the athletes, train special coaching staff, and finance research, maybe in areas like sports psychology for the handicapped. What do you think?''

"I think it's an incredible, worthwhile, ambitious, and altogether fabulous idea! And I can't think of anyone better than you to do it. It's a wonderful plan, Quinn,'' she finished softly. If someone had asked her a moment ago if she could possibly love this man more, she would have said no. Now she wasn't so sure.

"It'll be a lot of work and mean a lot of travel. Particularly in the first year or so. To be honest, the travel part doesn't exactly thrill me. I've been on enough planes to last me a lifetime. But it won't be forever and the cause is worth it—more than worth it. And with you along, it will be different. I'll want you to come with me, Emmi, as much as you can—as my wife.''

"Quinn, . . . what you're doing, it's wonderful, but it doesn't change things. It only points out again how wrong it would be for me to marry you. The life you describe will be so . . . populated, so social. You'll be meeting and wining and dining people all the time.

Maybe all over the world. I couldn't cope with that. I'd be a disaster for you and the foundation. You need a woman with presence, charisma. Besides, there's my writing. I know it may not seem like much, but it's important to me."

"It's important to me, too. I don't want you to give it up. I don't want you to give *anything* up. As for the social aspects, you can take part in as much or as little of it as you're comfortable with, but I want you with me. And for your information, you have more presence and charisma than a thousand women, but you refuse to see it. It's fear that holds you back, sweetheart, not inadequacies."

Emily wrapped herself in silence and stared into the dark waters lapping the shore. The lights came up on the stage of her mind. It was a party, peopled by a gold-clad cast, all reflecting light, shimmering as they moved confidently and easily about the room. She heard their laughter, admired them for their poise, their effortless conversation. She looked for herself; she was there—in the corner, silent and afraid, wearing olive drab. The scene she saw was not real, but the uneven palpitations in her chest were. She sighed long and deep.

Quinn had no idea what he was asking of her. Leave the island, her secure, comfortable existence, strike out in a new, strange direction? It was terrifying. Even the thought made her tremble. It would be exciting. She would see places in the world she never thought she'd see, and she would be with Quinn, but . . .

"I don't—" she started.

He turned her face to his and touched his fingers to her mouth. "For the moment, I think we've gone as far as words can take us. I'm going to be here for another two weeks. That should be enough time for you to get used to the idea.''

Emily fell silent again. *How can I tell him that two weeks, two years won't make any difference? That I will never be the woman he needs.*

Quinn stood up, took her hand, and pulled her to her feet. The soft night breeze fanned her drawn face. But it wasn't the breeze that made her shiver when Quinn's hands coasted over her shoulders and down her arms. Damn. She was going to cry. To stop the tears, she threw her arms around him and buried her face in his chest. Except for a hiccup, her ploy worked.

"You all right?" he asked pulling her closer.

"Fine." She burrowed deeper into his chest, not wanting to let him go. Tonight would see the last of loving, the fading shadows of passion. She was sure of it. She just didn't know how to tell him.

He stroked her hair. "You're cold, and probably damned tired. Go inside and get some sleep. I'll call you tomorrow."

She lifted her eyes to his. "Stay with me? Sleep with me?" *Make love to me, one more time*, she wanted to add but didn't.

"Just sleep? That's all you want?" He scanned her upturned face, his own expression reflective. "I don't think so. You want more than that and so do I. But the old rules don't apply anymore. We're a long way past easy island loving. If we make love tonight, it's a commitment. Is that understood?"

"Yes."

"And do you still want me to stay with you?"

"No." Emily lowered her head.

"I see." Quinn dropped his hands and took a step back.

Emily had never felt so alone, standing there with

his gaze fixed on her. Only a step away and it felt like a universe. It didn't matter. There was no way in the world she was going to marry Quinn Ramsay. She wasn't courageous enough.

"Understand, Quinn—please."

"Oh, I understand all right. Better than you think." His jaw tensed as he closed, then opened his mouth. "But there'll be no more stud service, Emily. Like I said, I'll call you tomorrow."

With that he was gone.

"Hello." Grace gripped the phone and peered at her alarm clock, blinking hard. Six A.M.!

"Will you take care of the store for a couple of weeks? I've already called Marsha. She says she can help out."

"Emily?" She sat up and flicked on the light. "What's going on? What's this about?"

"Please don't ask questions. I'm catching the first ferry to Crofton. I'm going up to Vancouver Island for a while. I'll be gone until . . . for at least two weeks. Will you look after things for me? And tell James I've taken Bailly with me, will you? He'll want to know."

"Emmi! What—"

"Grace, please . . ."

"Okay. But tell me this much. Does it have anything to do with that California man?"

"Sort of."

"Oh, Emmi, I told you. Didn't I tell you?"

"Will you do it . . . watch things for me?"

"You got it. But call. Okay?"

"Okay. Bye."

* * *

Quinn was at the bookstore when it opened at ten o'clock Monday morning. Grace saw him immediately as she turned the corner. He looked grim.

"Where is she?" he asked with no preamble.

Grace stepped past him to the door and put her key in the lock. "I take it you mean Emily."

"You take it right. Where the hell is she? I called before I went to see James in the relay yesterday. I called her when I got back. I drove over to her place last night, and it was locked up tight. Her car was gone."

Grace kept her tone breezy. "I think she decided to take a short holiday. You know, kind of a spur of the moment thing." Grace turned the key in the lock, opened the door, and looked at him over the curve of her shoulder.

His expression was cold and disbelieving. "And how long is this 'spur of the moment' holiday going to last? Did she say?"

"Two weeks or so."

Quinn's eyes were still on her, but Grace sensed he no longer saw her. He was motionless except for the jump of pain in his eyes. He quelled it with a shrug of broad shoulders and refocused on Grace.

"Will she be calling you?"

"I expect so." Grace tried to ignore his hurt and keep her tone light. There was nothing she could do— for either of them.

"When she does, tell her I get the message. And tell her she won't have to stay off her precious island for two weeks. I'm leaving tomorrow."

A week later, close to midnight, Emily pulled into her driveway. What moon there was lay behind heavy clouds, plump with rain. She wished she'd remembered to leave her porch light on. The night was unbroken black, and she stumbled twice during the dozen steps to her door. Not so Bailly, who was at the door in seconds, wagging and waiting for her to catch up.

"I'm glad one of us is happy to be home, Bailly."

She flicked on the light, dropped her suitcase at the door, and went into the kitchen.

"Water, fellah?"

As Bailly slurped noisily, Emily headed back to pick up her suitcase. She was tired but knew with certainty she would not sleep. Crossing back through the silent living room, she turned on another lamp. That was when she saw it.

The envelope was half under her case near the door. It said only EMMI in bold black caps. She knew immediately who it was from and sensed the beginning of another endless weep coming on. She stroked the envelope, then folded it. She didn't want to see the hard etch of his pen on white paper, didn't want to read his words, didn't want to suffer his loss again. She'd done the right thing.

"Emily?"

Emily's startled eyes flew to the slowly opening door. Her hand went to her chest, and the envelope fell to the rug.

"Sorry. I didn't mean to scare you." It was Lynn. "I saw the light, wasn't sure you were back, and decided to check. I wanted to talk to you." Lynn looked at her friend's ashen face. "Jeez, I did scare you, didn't I? I should have knocked."

"No. It's okay."

When Lynn cocked her head in question, Emily gave her a quick welcoming hug.

"Come in for a bit. I'm glad for the company. Coffee?"

"No, thanks." Lynn sat in the big chair near the fireplace. She looked determined. "How was the trip?"

"Good." Bailly flopped down beside Emmi, and she scratched behind her ears. "We needed those few days, didn't we, old guy?" Bailly gave her an adoring look, laid his head on his paws, and closed his eyes. Emmi turned back to face Lynn and pasted on a smile. "We went to Tofino to do some whale watching. It was great."

Lynn took in her pallid, drawn face. "Great, huh? You look more like you spent the week in Transylvania visiting the count. You look hellish, my dear. Pure and simply hellish. Almost as bad as that beautiful man you were so anxious to leave behind. That was a mistake, you know," Lynn finished softly.

"I did what was right for, uh, both of us."

"You were callous and insensitive. You were also cowardly. Quinn Ramsay is a special man. He didn't deserve that kind of treatment." Lynn spoke the words so matter-of-factly Emily didn't have time to be shocked. She went directly to anger.

"You know nothing about it, Lynn."

"I know you dished out the treatment you got years ago without batting an eyelash. I thought better of you." Lynn gave her an intense stare. "You ran, Emily Welland. And when you ran, you caused pain. Long-term pain, unless I miss my guess. My God, woman, that man loves you and you kicked him in the teeth."

"He told you that?"

"He told me nothing. He didn't have to. He came to say good-bye the day he left. He wanted to talk about a contract for James to be on promotional material for the foundation. He looked like . . . well, let's just say he looked as bad, if not worse, than you."

"I didn't want to hurt him. I never meant to."

"Well, you did."

"It wouldn't work, Lynn. We're too different."

"That's b.s. and you know it. But if you're determined it live behind that wall of fear you've created, so be it." Lynn shook her head, stood up, and headed for the door. She turned when she got there. "He's coming back in August, Emmi. To finalize the contract and talk to James about the games in Vancouver. Maybe, just maybe, you have another chance. If I were you, I'd take it."

Emily looked at her through pain-washed eyes and forced a tense smile to her lips. "You came here tonight expressly to give me what for, didn't you?"

Lynn nodded. "And I won't apologize for a word of it."

"You don't have to. I've spent the week clinging desperately to the idea that it wouldn't work for Quinn and me . . . that I'd made the right decision, done what was best for him. I *needed* to believe that." She smiled crookedly and used a knuckle to catch a tear at the top of her cheek. "And I was managing fine until you breezed in like the ghost of Christmas past and reminded me of what a fool I've been."

"You're not a fool. You just acted like one. There's a difference."

"That doesn't sound terribly logical, but I'll accept it anyway." The two women hugged before Lynn stepped outside. She turned back.

"By the way, that date in August? It's the second. In case you're interested. Make things right, Emily," she urged. "We all know that a second chance is hard to come by."

Emily closed the door and picked up the envelope. She tore it open.

Thanks for the "island love," Emily.
I'll miss you in my life.

Quinn

She checked the sob that threatened to burst from her throat. There would be no more bloody tears, she told herself. Not a drop, not a trickle, not a trace. She'd created this mess, so if she cried, it could only be for herself, and idiots didn't deserve tears. She read the note again.

"You will not miss me in your life, Quinn Ramsay. Not if I can undo the damage I've done. Not if you can forgive me my fear and stupidity. And not if I can find the courage to conquer them once and for all."

The quiet room accepted her fiercely whispered words and returned nothing. Bailly showed his indulgence by flicking one ear. Emily went to bed, dry eyed and resolute. But before she did, she filled in the August second square on her calendar with neon yellow highlighter.

As the ferry entered Fulford Harbour, Quinn walked to the right side of the boat. From here he would be able to see Lynn's place. James told him to watch for him, that he would be waving from the beach. That's what he would do, watch for James. He would not look at the house next door. The small cedar beach house where the woman he loved was planning to spend the rest of her life. It made his gut ache to come back here.

Thank God it wouldn't be for long. He'd talk to James, meet with Lynn, get the papers signed, and be gone in two hours. No man liked to return to the scene of his defeat. Who the hell needed a reminder? He saw James wave and waved back. After that no power on earth could stop him from looking at Emily's house. His heart stalled in his chest, then pumped erratically.

She was there, sitting on her log. He couldn't be sure, but it looked as if she was watching the ferry—watching him. He turned away, his rising anger and frustration telling him he didn't need this. When he was back in his car, he slammed his head against the headrest and let out a long breath. *Damn the woman!* he thought. Even seeing her from this distance made his blood race. If he could do it without being rude, he'd get off the island in an hour.

Emily stared at the ferry. Heart in throat, breath tight in chest, and hands knotted in her lap, she scanned the deck rails until she spotted him. Even though she couldn't make out his features, she knew the minute his eyes found her—the planet lurched. He was so close. She had thought of nothing but this day for two months, and still she had no plan. No idea what to do. The lines she'd composed vanished from her head at the sight of him. The curtain dropped on the scenes she'd created in her mind for the moment when she would see him again. Gone, all of it, gone. She would have to wing it. When he turned away from her, she swallowed deep. This was not going to be easy.

Rubbing her damp hands on the side of her jeans, she stood up. She was about to take the biggest risk of her life. She swallowed again and headed for the house. The ferry was at the dock. In minutes Quinn would be at Lynn's. Whatever plan she came up with in the next half hour or so would have to do. She had to see him before he left the island.

Quinn had barely completed the turn out of Lynn's driveway when he saw her. She was standing astride her bike, arms resting on the handlebars, in the middle of the country road. Bailly was beside her. Together they made an effective roadblock, and both woman and dog were looking at him. He stopped the car, studied them, but didn't turn off the ignition. He waited an eternity before pulling the car to the side of the road. It was another wait for him to get out of the car. When he walked toward her, all power and lean, toned muscle, Emily felt tossed and winded. She searched her mind frantically for a next move, a line of words, anything that would make sense.

"Hello, Emily," he said and waited.

She lifted her head and met his eyes. She could see the tension in them and her mouth went dry. She had no idea what to say.

"I have some strawberries." The inane comment spurted out from nowhere.

He didn't answer. What kind of response did a statement like that need anyway? He eyed her, one eyebrow raised in question as she tried again.

"I'm asking you to lunch."

"I've eaten."

"Oh." She ran her hands along the cool metal of the bike's handlebars. "How about a bike ride then?"

"I don't have a bike with me."

Silence.

He wasn't going to make this easy. She could see that. She fixed her gaze on him. It held a trace of frustration.

"A walk on the beach?" she asked.

"No time. I've got a ferry to catch."

Emily lowered her eyes and chewed on her lower lip. She bit too hard and winced. Quinn waited.

"Is that it then?" he asked.

"No." She wasn't letting him go yet. She was barely getting started.

"No?" he repeated, the barest hint of a smile touching his mouth before he quelled it. "You mean you have something more to offer, Emily?"

Her eyes flew up to his and a soft breath skimmed her lips. "I love you, Quinn Ramsay."

He took a step toward her. "How much, Emmi? How much do you love me?"

"Enough. Enough to go with you, be with you anywhere. Enough for . . . everything."

He reached for her then, pulling her to him roughly, the cold metal of the bike an unyielding fence between them.

His mouth hovered over hers and she heard him curse. "Damn you, woman. You'd better not run scared on me again. I won't be responsible for my actions if you get cold feet on me again. I love you, Emily. I want you. I need you. All of it, damn it." His gaze was fierce, demanding.

She took courage from the strong beat of his heart and smiled into his eyes. "No running. I promise. And if you marry me, I'll probably never have cold feet again."

The breath caught in Quinn's throat at her words, and he gave her a loving and very sexy smile. "Not in my bed, you won't. I promise you won't have cold anything. You have my word on it." He pulled back and his expression turned serious. "And I promise that I'll always be there for you, Emmi. At your side, loving and caring for you with all my heart."

His kiss, when it came, broke her in pieces and put her together again. She strained to get closer, ignoring the sharp jab of the bike's handlebars. He slanted his head to deepen the kiss and their bodies instantly re-

sponded to a newer, deeper beat. Quinn's hand coursed
up her shoulders to rest at the base of her throat. She
could feel their heat and strength through her thin
blouse. When he groaned and pulled back, his eyes met
hers with a smile and a promise. The smile was for the
moment, the promise for a lifetime.

EPILOGUE

After dinner, the three women spread themselves comfortably around Emily's cozy living room. Grace sprawled on the sofa, Lynn took the rocking chair beside the fireplace, and Emily curled into the old wing-back. Each held a steaming, convivial cup of coffee while outside the moon hovered low, quietly silvering the waters of Fulford Harbour. Bailly wandered in, surveyed the room's inhabitants, and promptly curled up at Emily's feet.

Emily and Lynn were comfortable in the silence. Grace was not.

"So," she began, "when exactly does that heavenly California man of yours get back?"

"He is heavenly, isn't he?" Emily's eyes strayed to the moon outside the window as she sighed softly.

Grace looked at Lynn, rolled her eyes, and smiled. Lynn smiled back.

"Hello! Earth to Emily. Come in, please," Grace said.

Emily's sheepish eyes looked from friend to friend.

"Sorry, Quinn's due back Friday morning. But I'm not going to see him before the wedding," she added, ruing their agreed upon plan. She couldn't bear to think of his being on the island and not with her—not even for one night. He'd been gone almost two weeks now, and it seemed a lifetime.

Grace sipped her coffee. "You mean he's not going to be here until the day before the wedding? He's really pushing it, isn't he?"

"I guess, but as it turned out, he didn't have much choice. There are meetings on the sale of his business, and what with everyone's schedules, they were impossible to delay. And I think things are moving faster for the foundation than he expected. It looks like he's made a good connection in France for games as early as next year."

"May second to ninth, according to James," Lynn added with a proud grin, "and you know he's never wrong about dates."

"You heard from him?" Emily asked.

"Yesterday. I guess they called me right after Quinn talked to you. James is having the time of his life in Los Angeles. That man of yours has been wonderful with him. He's been to Disneyland, on a studio tour, and to a wax museum of some kind. He was so excited I barely understood him. He said he missed me, but I think Quinn had to remind him to say it," Lynn groused but looked pleased.

Grace chimed in. "The little traitor. Seduced by the bright lights and big city. Huh?"

"That's about it," Lynn said, smiling at Grace across the rim of her coffee cup.

Emily sat up a little straighter in the chair, worry wrinkling her brow. "You're going to be okay with this, uh, arrangement, aren't you, Lynn?"

Lynn's brown eyes turned serious. "How can you even ask, Emily? It's the opportunity of a lifetime for James. Official spokesman for the Marion Foundation. My son. Can you believe it?"

"He'll be away a lot," Emily said. "Quinn wants him to be an integral part of the foundation. You'll be lonely."

Lynn's eyes leveled to meet hers. "I haven't loved that boy all these years, challenged him until at times he should have hated me, to let a little loneliness stand in his way now. His world—my God—his *skills* are growing everyday. My damn heart just about bursts thinking of it. I'm so proud, I— Well, anyway, Quinn is good for him, and it's time he spent more time around men."

Grace piped up. "Ditto for you, kiddo. And me."

"You've got a one-track mind, Grace. Has anybody ever told you that?" Emily teased.

"And as for me," Lynn added, "a man is the last thing I'm looking for."

"Hah! The first comment from a woman who's made the biggest catch of this century without even fishing, and the second from a woman who hasn't so much as glanced at a member of the male sex, other than that handsome son of hers, for fifteen years." Grace threw up her hands in mock surrender. "With friends like this, no wonder I'm single. You guys are no help at all. I give up. That's all. I'm quitting, throwing in the towel."

Lynn lifted her gaze to heaven and Emily gave a delicate snort. They both grinned.

"Very dramatic, Grace, but I think there's as much chance of you calling off your manhunt as there is of my starting one," Lynn said, dryly.

"True," Grace admitted without guile. "But then, I

really can't help myself. I'm a very focused person. But hey, enough about me, let's talk about Em's wedding—and what *I'm* going to wear," she finished airily.

"It's a wonderful idea to get married on the beach, Emily," Lynn said, her voice filled with enthusiasm. "It will be a perfect background."

"*If* the weather holds," Emily added. "If it doesn't, we'll go inside. The guest list is pretty small, so Paul's house will easily handle us all."

Lynn shook her head thoughtfully. "Who would have believed it? Shy Emily Welland—a September bride."

"It feels like some kind of miracle," Emily added dreamily, envisioning her husband to be. She couldn't think about him without being claimed by a hazy swirl of passion. His eyes, mouth, the thickness of his sunglazed dark hair, his teasing smile—and now his ambition for the foundation. They all merged and layered to create the man she loved—with all her shy but courageous heart. She stared unseeing into the cool coffee at the bottom of her cup, warming in the image, the certainty of what they would have together.

"Yoo-hoo! Emily," Lynn nudged her with the toe of her shoe.

Grace stood up in mock exasperation. "It's no use, Lynn. It's time to go. The woman is completely gone. I don't think we can expect an intelligent conversation out of her for at least a year. She's crazy in love. That's what she is."

Grace smiled down at Emily, and her words no longer teased when she said, "Not that I blame you, Emmi. He's truly wonderful."

As Emily stood, Grace grabbed her into a rough, affectionate hug. "But then so are you. And don't you ever forget it." Her grip tightened, and she swallowed hard before releasing her. "I love you, Em. See you at the wedding." Giving Emily no time to respond, Grace all but ran out of the room.

Emily and Lynn sniffed in unison as they watched her go. Lynn wiped quietly under an eye before picking up her sweater and draping it loosely over her shoulders.

The room fell into silence.

Lynn coughed lightly as though to ease a tight throat. "I'd better go too. Tonight—dinner for the three of us—it was a good idea, Em. It's been a long time. Thanks for— Oh, dammit, anyway." Lynn's voice broke and she wrapped her arms around her. Her sweater fell to the floor forgotten. "I'm going to miss you *so much*. It's going to be awful that you're not here. You're my best—my very dearest—friend."

For a long moment the two women clung to each other and let tears fall unchecked down their cheeks.

When they drew apart, Emily held Lynn's hands and looked deep into her eyes. "I love you both, you and Grace, but if it hadn't been for you, Lynn—being there, listening," she smiled softly, "prodding me to move on, urging me to take risks, I might never have—"

"Hush." Lynn touched Emily's mouth with her finger. "The universe unfolded as it should. Out of all the islands in the world, Quinn Ramsay came to Salt Spring—for you, Emily—to find you. It was meant to be."

Emily could find no words to reply but wished with all her heart that her friend would find the kind of happiness she had.

Composed now, they hugged each other again and said their good nights. Both knew it would not be goodbye.

* * *

"You are *not* supposed to be here. We agreed." Emily folded into Quinn's arms like a weary traveler, her actions completely at odds with her chastising words. "Oh, Quinn, I missed you so."

She raised her lips to his, and he kissed her fully, deeply, pulling back before passion ensnared them both. They would wait.

"I had to see you if only for a minute." He grinned and stroked her cheek. "I wanted to be sure you hadn't run out on me."

Emily smiled back. "I already tried that." She shook her head. "Didn't like it, not even a little bit. I'm afraid you're stuck with me."

"Thank God for that, because tomorrow you become my wife and then—" He pulled her deeper into the embrace and whispered in her ear.

Emily laughed and pulled away. She was slightly breathless. "Promises, promises," she said. "Now go, my wild lover. I'll see you at our wedding."

He kissed her again and let out a jagged breath. "This is tough, Emmi. I don't want to leave." He nibbled her earlobe. "You don't *really* want me to leave. Do you?"

Emily could scarcely breath. Her heart beat staccato in her chest. His heat infused her, blocking reason and wreaking havoc on her well-made plans. She wanted him to stay . . . but she absolutely had to do some last-minute work on her dress. "Quinn, we agreed," she mumbled into his shoulder.

He shuddered, pulled her tight against him, then let her go. He lifted his eyes skyward. "I'm a saint."

Emily's lips twisted into a grin. "After what you just whispered in my ear? I don't think so. Now *go!*"

After he'd gone, she noticed a large parcel near the front door. There was a card. She opened it.

Emmi: This is not your wedding present, so open it. It's for high-flyin' words. I love you.

Quinn

It was a portable computer.

Saturday morning the sun joined the celebration. And while the air tingled with the promise of fall, the day was crystalline. Quinn and Emily stood on the shore and spoke their vows. Family, friends, and the music of the ocean tide formed the background.

Quinn kissed his bride with a sense of wonder. Pulling back, he looked down at her, watched her smile grow and deepen as she met his gaze. I love you, she mouthed, for his eyes only. Silent words for his hungry heart. His chest constricted almost painfully. It was done. This island woman with the rain-colored eyes was finally his. She had given him her love and her trust, and he was bound to her, happily and forever.

As one, they turned to the small gathering of friends waiting to wish them well.

An hour later, Quinn sat blessedly and contentedly alone on Paul's deck. He was watching Emily as she laughed and mingled with her friends. She looked relaxed and happy.

"It's trite, but it has to be said. You're a lucky man, Ramsay." Paul stepped up beside him, his gaze following Quinn's. "She's beautiful—inside and out." He took a drink from the glass in his hand.

Quinn smiled. "That she is," he said, before pulling his eyes from his bride and turning them toward his friend.

He cocked an eyebrow and tilted his head. "Gina?" he asked.

"Gone," Paul answered.

Quinn nodded his head.

Paul leaned against the railing and crossed his long legs. "I'm going to take your advice. Go cold turkey. No more women for a while—a long while."

Quinn couldn't stop his grin.

"What's so funny?"

"Nothing, I was just thinking that not too many months ago I felt the same way—and look at me."

The men exchanged grins.

Emily came up behind Quinn, wrapped her arms around his waist, and nestled her head between his shoulder blades. She glanced up at Paul. "Can I steal my newly minted husband for a minute? I want him to meet someone special, do you mind?" She slipped around to stand at Quinn's side, and Paul bent to kiss her forehead.

"Take him away, Emily. Officially, the man is all yours," he teased.

"Emily, Mrs. Duncan is leaving and she wants to say good-bye." Lynn came up beside her.

"Oh, that's who I want you to meet, Quinn," Emily said. "Will you look after Paul, Lynn?"

Lynn smiled in Paul's direction. "Give me an introduction and I'll be happy to," she said.

Emily looked back. "Didn't you meet . . . at my play opening? Oh—that's right—you weren't there. I'm sorry. Lynn, this is Paul Severns, Quinn's friend from Los Angeles. Paul directs movies." With that she and Quinn turned to find Mrs. Duncan.

Paul and Lynn smiled after them and at each other.

"They're going to make it, aren't they?" Paul lifted his glass in the direction of the retreating couple.

Their gazes locked briefly before Lynn followed his gesture. He looked deeply thoughtful, almost—wistful.

Lynn got a little wistful herself when Quinn pulled Emily close and bent his head to speak in her ear. The gesture was intimate and loving. A breeze came up from the ocean carrying Emily's quiet laughter back to where Paul and Lynn stood on the deck.

A lump formed in Lynn's throat and her eyes misted as she contemplated the happy couple. "Oh, yes. They'll make it," she whispered, as much to herself as to Paul.

SHARE THE FUN . . .
SHARE YOUR NEW-FOUND TREASURE!!

You don't want to let your new books out of your sight? That's okay. Your friends can get their own. Order below.

No. 89 JUST ONE KISS by Carole Dean
Michael is Nikki's guardian angel and too handsome for his own good.

No. 111 CALIFORNIA MAN by Carole Dean
Quinn had the Midas touch in business but Emily was another story.

No. 88 MORE THAN A MEMORY by Lois Faye Dyer
Cole and Melanie both still burn from the heat of that long ago summer.

No. 90 HOLD BACK THE NIGHT by Sandra Steffen
Shane is a man with a mission and ready for anything . . . except Starr.

No. 91 FIRST MATE by Susan Macias
It only takes a minute for Mac to see that Amy isn't so little anymore.

No. 92 TO LOVE AGAIN by Dana Lynn Hites
Cord thought just one kiss would be enough. But Honey proved him wrong!

No. 93 NO LIMIT TO LOVE by Kate Freiman
Lisa was called the "little boss" and Bruiser didn't like it one bit!

No. 94 SPECIAL EFFECTS by Jo Leigh
Catlin wouldn't fall for any tricks from Luke, the master of illusion.

No. 95 PURE INSTINCT by Ellen Fletcher
She tried but Amie couldn't forget Buck's strong arms and teasing lips.

No. 96 THERE IS A SEASON by Phyllis Houseman
The heat of the volcano rivaled the passion between Joshua and Beth.

No. 97 THE STILLMAN CURSE by Peggy Morse
Leandra thought revenge would be sweet. Todd had sweeter things in mind.

No. 98 BABY MAKES FIVE by Lacey Dancer
Cait could say 'no' to his business offer but not to Robert, the man.

No. 99 MOON SHOWERS by Laura Phillips
Both Sam and the historic Missouri home quickly won Hilary's heart.

No. 100 GARDEN OF FANTASY by Karen Rose Smith
If Beth wasn't careful, she'd fall into the arms of her enemy, Nash.

No. 101 HEARTSONG by Judi Lind
From the beginning, Matt knew Lainie wasn't a run-of-the-mill guest.

No. 102 SWEPT AWAY by Cay David
Sam was insufferable . . . and the most irresistible man Charlotte ever met.

No. 103 FOR THE THRILL by Janis Reams Hudson
Maggie hates cowboys, *all* cowboys! Alex has his work cut out for him.

No. 104 SWEET HARVEST by Lisa Ann Verge
Amanda never mixes business with pleasure but Garrick has other ideas.

No. 105 SARA'S FAMILY by Ann Justice
Harrison always gets his own way . . . until he meets stubborn Sara.

No. 106 TRAVELIN' MAN by Lois Faye Dyer
Josh needs a temporary bride. The ruse is over, can he let her go?

No. 107 STOLEN KISSES by Sally Falcon
In Jessie's search for Mr. Right, Trevor was definitely a wrong turn!

No. 108 IN YOUR DREAMS by Lynn Bulock
Meg's dreams become reality when Alex reappears in her peaceful life.

No. 109 HONOR'S PROMISE by Sharon Sala
Once Honor gave her word to Trace, there would be no turning back.

No. 110 BEGINNINGS by Laura Phillips
Abby had her future completely mapped out—until Matt showed up.

Meteor Publishing Corporation
Dept. 1092, P. O. Box 41820, Philadelphia, PA 19101-9828

Please send the books I've indicated below. Check or money order (U.S. Dollars only)—no cash, stamps or C.O.D.s (PA residents, add 6% sales tax). I am enclosing $2.95 plus 75¢ handling fee for *each* book ordered.

Total Amount Enclosed: $_____.

____ No. 89	____ No. 93	____ No. 99	____ No. 105
____ No. 111	____ No. 94	____ No. 100	____ No. 106
____ No. 88	____ No. 95	____ No. 101	____ No. 107
____ No. 90	____ No. 96	____ No. 102	____ No. 108
____ No. 91	____ No. 97	____ No. 103	____ No. 109
____ No. 92	____ No. 98	____ No. 104	____ No. 110

Please Print:
Name _____
Address _____ Apt. No. _____
City/State _____ Zip _____

Allow four to six weeks for delivery. Quantities limited.